# RABID CHANGE

Barry Magrill

ISBN-13: 9798614486518
ISBN-10: B084Q9WPN5

Cover design by: Art Painter
Library of Congress Control Number: 2018675309
Printed in the United States of America

*For Judy, Jamie, Haley and Geoffrey and MomnDad*

# Rabid Change

## Barry Magrill

Prologue

Toy crawled shakily along the cold metal beam of the Ferris wheel, fifteen feet above the rapidly churning water. Halfway to reaching the gondola car at the wheel's outer rim his knee slipped out from under him. Automatically he hugged the thick blue spoke with his spindly arms and legs to avoid falling into the water. This felt like second grade all over again, when he naïvely climbed to the top of the school Twirly Slide and fell over the railing, only to be saved by the lowest crossbar catching him between the legs. If you can call that being saved. That was four grades ago and he was still afraid of heights. Water was a whole other problem.

Water wasn't supposed to be under the ride. Yet, here he was stuck on a Ferris wheel that stopped moving long ago, that he agreed to ride merely to prove a point. And on top of it all he was in an amusement park where everybody was supposed to be happy, yet completely surrounded by the thing he hated the most. Ocean.

Toy looked down at the water beneath him, to where his parents should be waiting for him around the base of the ride. They were gone. Deep water had rushed in and covered everything. No idea what happened to them. Were they swept out to the big sea that brushed up against the amusement park? He wanted to think that they managed to save themselves by outrunning the water. But, what he remembered was already blurry, tearing at the edges. Without a clear recollection he focused on the moment. Now. And what he knew was that among all the rides in the amusement park and the shops, trees, and lamp posts only the Ferris wheel, twenty storeys tall, was still above the dark green water. Water as far as the horizon covered the lower third of the giant wheel. Toy was stuck and it felt like no one was coming.

## Hot Water

Clinging to the blue spoke of the massive Ferris wheel, afraid of falling into the ocean that waited below him, Toy was paralyzed. Lost. He recalled being lost the very first time. When he was really little Momndad took him to Kiddieland. He was excited about the rocketship ride that went in slow circles around a flashing red light. In the line were only a few kids. Toy badly wanted to ride the gold rocket and so he stood there in line worrying that one of the few kids ahead of him would take it first. He was ashamed to say out loud that he wanted it, in case they'd take it just to spite him. So he stayed silent, waiting to run ahead of the other kids when the gate opened. If he could get there first. At first he was happy that he got the gold rocketship but then instantly felt ashamed without knowing why. He could see the other kids didn't care anyway. Their smiling faces, laughing with each other as though they were laughing at Toy, etched themselves into his mental picture of the moment. By the time the ride started moving he was already thinking ahead to the next ride. So, when it ended he wandered off without Momndad to the Merry-go-Round and climbed onto one of the stationary horses. He felt the sun warm his face and the speed from the ride rustle his brown curly hair. He was feeling pretty grown up for going on the ride all by himself. Momndad would be proud, too. But when the music stopped no one was waiting at the exit gate. At first he just stood there. Frozen. After a minute of panic he began looking for them and weaving through an ocean of grownups. He was drowning in an endless pool of adult legs. A huge hole, like a drain, opened in his chest that sucked all of the air out of his lungs. It was the dread, the same dread he felt when his stomach fell out from under him on the swings. He couldn't breathe. He lacked the strength to cry out. He turned in every direction and saw only strangers. Their blank faces like horrid uncaring masks. Cold and lost felt exactly the same. Hollowed out, he stared into space. Motionless.

It was a mystery how they found him, something he never bothered to question. All of a sudden Momndad were simply there above him. "Next time", they said in agitation, "just wait in one place and we'll find you. If you go running off we won't be able to find you." He remembered thinking one thing only. There's going to be a next time? But he was too ashamed to ask out loud.

This time around the panic was deeper. Afraid to venture on the beam any further he crawled back to the safety of his Ferris wheel gondola car where he had started, completely dejected. In the pit of his stomach was a huge cold knot that quickly spread to the rest of his thin body. He shivered, sitting in the gondola, though the air was actually hot. Looking out of the mesh enclosed car, he could see that the surface of the water was covered by a carpet of plastic. Bottles, floating cushions, large jagged bits of broken wood and other pieces of plastic in a rainbow of colours. Pink, baby blue, coral, lemon yellow. No green plastic, though. Deep green was the colour of the water in the few holes forming and closing like little mouths in the undulating plastic carpet. And weaving through it all, connecting the water bottles to everything else was a very thin black ribbon. It linked a numberless wave of bottles. An endless sea of floating half-empty water bottles. Undulating. Undulating like the rocket patterned bedsheet fabric waves that Toy's mom flipped up in the air with a flick of her wrist when she made his bed in the morning. When Toy was really little they played a game of him leaping under the rising and falling cotton fabric. But he was never going to dive beneath the surface of this plastic carpet because he panicked around water. Even the sandy beach made him cringe. He almost never put his face in the water. So here he was, stuck between both of his fears trapped on a Ferris wheel, confined between the big ocean and the American Sea.

He thought back to how he got here. Water had just showed up out of nowhere while he sat on the Ferris wheel. There was really no warning. It was as though he blinked and the park pavement, rolling grass hills, and colourful stucco buildings that sold cotton candy were all completely submerged. Water as far as he

4

could see, off into the fog on the horizon. A magical cocoon of fog surrounding the ride.

Earlier, he had chosen Ferris wheel car number 13-C to ride alone. He didn't want to be with strangers in case he freaked out. He wondered if that was why the Mercury astronauts went up one at a time. So they didn't freak out and start to fight with each other. He often wondered if they were lonesome on their journey. And before their miraculous flight, ahead of them on the other side of the world, the Russian Gagarin soloed in space. Grinning the whole way, he defied the odds only to die in a fiery test flight less than ten years on. At least he wasn't alone on that final maneuver. Toy identified with the lone astronaut circling the planet at the furthest distance. Most of the time he didn't want to be around other people, anyway. He didn't like to talk with other kids because he was never sure how to answer the things that they said. So, when the Ferris wheel attendant had casually asked, "are you a single?", Toy answered "yep" so quickly that his word stood on the toes of the boy's sentence. Feeling even more uncomfortable, Toy was assigned the next free car that came along. Number 13. The boy looked at him in doubt as though to say, "are you really old enough to ride this by yourself?" To Toy it looked as though the attendant wasn't really into operating the ride at all. Never a good sign. He'd probably been working there all season so he saw thousands of people ride. All of them began to resemble the same person. Brown shorts, Rush t-shirt, hat purchased in the park, and beaten up runners. His only job, and it was a boring one, was to sort out the singles from the paired riders and put them in the proper cars. Toy guessed the boy's mind was really on meeting up with friends after the park closed to guzzle beer out back. Did any of the other employees really care about the park? What was on their minds as they watched the same ride go in circles all day long and into the night? Caring for the rides and everything else was a job for somebody else. No one saw Toy detour into the special line for the looping gondola cars, the ones that weren't affixed to the outer rim of the Ferris wheel. This meant that his car swung back and forth along a looping track as the giant wheel rotated. Toy had observed before he got in line that the inner cars didn't go as high up as the outer ones. That was fine with Toy. The Ferris wheel was so tall that the outer cars were way out of his comfort zone. But he'd agreed to conquer his fears so it was this or the damn rollercoaster. If he stuck to the inner gondolas he'd never get trapped at the very top while people got off and on. That was the simple plan. Get on, do five revolutions and hop off. Easy.

The Ferris wheel had made four trips around and in one more it would have been over. On the fourth time around, the ride had stopped to let some riders off. The ground was a few minutes away when the water came barreling in like a roller-coaster.

The ocean came without any warning. No, that was untrue. First, the music all over the park had gone off suddenly. That non-stop music you heard on the rides, in the restaurants, and even in the bathrooms. People stopped for a moment because the silence was jarring. But nobody knew what to do. They stood there like statues. Next, the power went off all over the park and the Ferris wheel stopped with a grinding shake. By then, everyone took no-tice of the park's stillness. And Toy had been so close to getting off, too. He could see Momndad waiting at the ride's exit gate. Their faces blank stares. Impassioned. Just flatly looking up at him. Did they turn and walk away, hand in hand? What were they doing? Did they see the water coming while he did not, when he was up so high he should have seen it coming, himself? He didn't see anybody swept away. He didn't see anything. He was stuck, unblinking eyes seeing only his thoughts. When he zoned out like this it was like seeing everything from a distance, like through a pin-hole camera. And he was trapped inside the little camera box until the episode ended. When the world finally rushed back in and normal returned he realized the rushing water wasn't like the tsunami footage he'd seen on the Internet a year earlier on that island somewhere. The horrible beach. The water didn't come crashing in like a surfer's wave. It just rolled in like the time he left the bath water running and it overflowed onto the tile floor.

So high it lifted his red bathtub boat and floated it away. He sat in the bath, waiting. As though the water would turn itself off. Like then, the water just rose higher and higher. He stared down at the rising water, blankly watching it rise closer and closer to his gondola. His heart raced with the sensation of water rising to his chin. The sudden swell slowed about eight feet from the bottom of his car and slowly undulated in silence. When he saw it had stopped rising he calmed. For a very brief moment it seemed as innocent as a park pond on Sunday afternoon.

No birds chirped. No people screamed. No music. Only the deep green water. Forever. He stared into its silence. It was empty and he felt nothing at all. Nothing. Just when he thought it would never change, that the cushion of water was going to sit there for eternity, the water suddenly reversed direction and sound came rushing back.

At first it sounded like mooing. Like a chorus of cows mooing. A short laugh escaped his lips. The mooing got louder and louder. Crushingly loud. He covered his ears to the groaning of ruptured metal. It wasn't mooing anymore but instead a chorus of dying, screaming cows performing a horrendous concert. The twang of something brittle snapped. The Ferris wheel shuddered side to side. That's when the green water became covered by a layer of floating plastic as if the trash cans all over the park had erupted in mini volcanoes. Last year in fifth grade he'd made a volcano for a science project. In truth Momndad made it and he watched as they shaped the cone and filled it with soda or whatever. It was supposed to erupt spectacularly at the science fair but in fact there was more of an oozing over the edges than an explosion. It got honorable mention. And this was how the water moved around the Ferris wheel. When it pulled back, the water level only went down a couple of feet and the carpet of plastic garbage settled in for good. An honorable mention of disasters, mostly silent and boring. It certainly wasn't a volcano.

After staring into the carpet for hours Toy could still not figure out if it was rising higher by tiny increments or not. He couldn't see far enough into the future to know if it was a threat.

He knew one thing for sure, he was getting hungry.

Gondola Car 13

A few minutes into the terrifying Ferris wheel ride, the whole machine stopped abruptly and Toy was momentarily relieved. He sat motionlessly on the padded seat expecting the door to open. He was ready to run onto the exit ramp, faking that he had enjoyed the ride. He didn't do either. The door didn't open. He sat there completely still. Afraid to move in case the slightest adjustment to the balance of the gondola might tip the whole Ferris wheel crashing down. He was so still that he forgot to breathe. At last he sucked in some air deeply and shifted his lean body a little. Relieved, the car did not budge.

He worked up the courage to curl up on the seat, slowly laying on his side, looking over at the empty bench across from him. When Toy had entered the gondola car to ride the Ferris wheel for the very first time he was more than excited, panicked almost. But he was holding the panic in like a huge gulp of air that was too big for his wiry body. The moment the ride started moving for the first time with him in it, he knew he'd made a terrible mistake. As the huge wheel of the ride revolved, the gondola car swung wildly along its looping track in long and drawn out motions. His stomach objected to such random movements. Toy felt sick immediately and he worried he might blank out. He had blanked out before for no reason, not remembering where he had been or what he'd been doing. That would have been a blessing but instead he was wide awake. The car was going in two directions at once, up-out and then down-back. Instead of looking out at the view of the park, he stared at the thin wire mesh that enclosed the upper part of the open-air gondola car. The mesh extended from the top of the padded bench all the way up to the roof of the car, making it seem like a birdcage. A prison. A wildly swinging people prison. The mesh was pretty solid. He reached up to touch it.

That was the moment everything changed.

He was still looking at the mesh, not the amusement park, when the water rushed in. He was still ignoring the water when his thoughts turned to escaping from the gondola. The only obvious way out was the way he came in, through the sliding double doors on either side of the car. "How do I open these? The guy locked the lever when I got on." Toy's gondola was about two storeys above the water's surface, too high for a rescuer from below. The only rescue would be attempted by helicopter. And sitting in silence, Toy wondered if anybody was coming. There was not a single sound of anyone at all. No sirens. No loudspeakers. No alarms. That's why he hadn't bothered calling for help. It seemed like no one was out there. No helicopters, no search parties, no nothing. Only water.

Getting out of the gondola would not solve everything. But it was a start. Toy became fixated on the one thing that seemed important. Escape from his cage.

Pulling the doors apart seemed his only option. With a great deal of strain, as much as he could muster, he managed to open them up a few inches. They didn't open more than that no matter how hard he pushed and pulled. And even when he jammed his arm in the thin space between the sliding doors and tried to pry it open he couldn't even fit his head in there.

"I'm not that skinny".

While his arm was reaching outside it searched for any kind of latch that might part the doors. A safety latch. But he only felt the smooth surface of the metal gondola. He tried for an eternity but finally gave up and sat down on the floor. In frustration he looked up as if searching for an answer and saw his salvation in a terrifying instant. There was an emergency trap door in the roof he didn't notice before. It reminded him of the little doors of the wooden elevators in the old building where Momndad worked. He visited their office a few times on the sixth floor. The elevator door had to be opened and closed manually but it was modern enough that it had a bank of round black plastic buttons to choose the floor you wanted. The button snapped into place and the elevator lurched up with a rattle. "Getting out of that old elevator was a crap-shoot", Momndad used to say with a smile because the floor of the thing never perfectly matched up exactly with the floor of the building. A step up or down of six inches was always needed. Toy always worried that the elevator would break down completely while he was in it and being the smallest person among adults, he'd be elected to climb through the tiny, mysterious door in the roof of the elevator to go for help. It never happened except in his imagination. He guessed it was pitch black up there and that there were cables and mechanical things that pinched if you touched them. The escape route in the elevator seemed to Toy like a false sense of hope because once you were on the top of the elevator you were still stuck in the pitch black shaft with no way out. Only dirtier.

The elevator nightmare finally came true. After a long while he finally got up the nerve to reach for the handle over his head and pull. It didn't budge. The stubborn handle wouldn't budge. Toy went from surprise to anger in a split second. It wasn't the result he expected and that made him mad, blaming the handle for being stuck. It dared prevent him from getting outside. He didn't really think through what freedom from the gondola meant. So, he grabbed the handle with both hands and hung from it with all of his slim weight. Still nothing. He swung side to side and suddenly it released with a metallic snap, sending him crashing to the floor. The hatch popped open. The sky was visible through the little opening. He could easily fit through the small hole but it took him a long, long, long time until he got up the nerve to climb. What terrified him was the idea of standing on top of the gondola, on such a tiny platform without a railing to hold. Worse than falling he feared that sensation of almost falling. The pre-fall. That feeling he had in a dream when he was just starting to fall from a great height, and there was nothing to grab hold of. That feeling of the inevitability of falling. That nothing could stop it. It was terrible to feel the fall coming and to be helpless to stop it. All he could do was close his eyes. When he opened them again he was resolved to just poke his head through the hole and see what was there. He could see that to his right, the track that the car ran along was within an easy reach so, in fact, he could stand on the roof and hold onto the bar for balance.

Climbing through the hole very slowly, he pulled himself flat on his stomach on the roof to get used to the feeling. Holding the metal track he rose by inches to a shaky but standing position, feeling dizzy from seeing the open water below. Near him was the blue metal spoke of the Ferris wheel about a foot or two thick. It was easy to reach so he could climb down toward the water without too much trouble. It was more of a gentle descent, really. But once he got to the water there was nowhere to go since it seemed like the beam he was on simply disappeared. Too deep for him to swim. He'd always stayed in the shallow end in the pool so he could stand on his tip toes and still keep his head bone dry. He didn't have to see into this water to know that it was too deep for him to touch the bottom. On the surface, in the carpet of garbage and half empty water bottles connected to one another by the impossibly thin black ribbon, he saw bags of other things. Carmel Corn.

Toy crawled feet first down the blue metal beam that he named after the letters stenciled on its side, x-33. As he neared the water it was clear that there was a submerged gondola whose roof he could stand upon in water up to his ankles. It was like being on a raft floating a few inches underwater. Reaching out for the bags of Carmel Corn was exciting because he also found other bags of food among the garbage that was vomited up from the concession stands. He fished out as many of the bags as he could from the carpet of plastic and climbed back up to his car. Popcorn, red licorice, marshmallow Rice Krispies squares in the shape of animals, and beef jerky. He opened the popcorn first and finished it in a few minutes. Then half a package of beef jerky. Finally, he opened a bottle of water. He paused before drinking and looking out at the carpet of bottles bobbing in the gentle waves. Which one of these bottles, he wondered, held a genie. If he could find that one bottle, he knew exactly what he would use his three wishes for.

He had spent most of the day going up and down an eight foot incline from the gondola tree house to the carpet, picking out more packages of Carmel Corn, Hot Rods, and half empty water bottles. And Kinder Eggs. Lots of Kinder Eggs floating along the surface of the plastic carpet like musical notes punctuating the score of an ocean sized symphony. So many eggs. Removing a lifetime supply of Kinder Eggs couldn't even put a dent in the floating layer of garbage. Fishing things out of the water became a game. When he pulled something out of the water it seemed like he was taking a jigsaw piece away from a finished puzzle, except the empty hole closed up almost right away. By sunset he filled the seat of the gondola with bags and bags of the things Momndad liked to call 'crap'. Stuff he would almost never be allowed to eat became the entire contents of his little pantry. As he watched the sun hit the water for the first time in his life, imagining that he heard it steam, he started back on the Carmel Corn.

Eggs

Toy liked eggs. Real eggs. He could still taste the eggs he ordered in the hotel restaurant the day before yesterday. The eggs came in two tiny white cups, which he'd thought everyone called 'eggies in a cup' except the waitress didn't know what he meant until Momndad intervened. "Soft boiled", she said. He hacked away at the egg shell with a dull stainless steel knife trying to expose the plump yolk floating in the pool of white. In frustration with the table knife, he wanted to resort to the folding jackknife he got for his last birthday but Momndad made him keep it in his pocket with his magnifying glass. One of the knife's blades could surely cut eggs. In the end, the eggs were cracked opened for him with a spoon because the amusement park wouldn't wait all day. In fact, the whole point of the late lunch was to eat something easily digestible before going on the most important ride. The Ferris wheel. The last thing Toy wanted was to get sick on the ride. It was going to be his very first time going on the ride by himself. He really wasn't ready.

The rides that Toy had been on up to that point never required a meal plan. It didn't matter what he put in his mouth before going on the merry-go-round, the bumper cars, or the haunted house. He didn't think twice about those. They weren't hero rides. But the Ferris wheel was different. He'd been fascinated by it since he was very, very little. Since the time he was too small to ride it at all. The sight of the giant wheel attracted and terrified him. You could see it long before you entered the park, monumentally towering over the tallest trees. The picture of that huge revolving wheel, lit at night with three and a half thousand glowing lights like the stars turning in the black sky was burned into his mind. Seeing him awestruck by the glowing Ferris wheel the very first time he went to a fair with Momndad they said in unison, "one day you'll be big enough to ride it. Just you wait." In fact, Toy was happy to wait. He was in no hurry. His fascination wasn't wrapped up in anticipation but dread. And yet it's coming was inevitable. On the morning he was going to climb into the gondola car of the Ferris wheel he had a knot in his stomach the size of an egg.

Toy's obsession with the Ferris wheel started the summer that Jungle John the morning radio jock on the local station broke the record for riding one. Thirty-eight days. It was a stunt to promote the station. He lived on it day and night. They even enclosed his open seat with a special canopy to keep the rain off Jungle John. It also prevented anyone from seeing him lay down in there, sleeping most of the day and night. The outside was imprinted with the radio station's call sign, KLNG-101, and a big cartoon of Jungle John's smiling face. The awning became a version of Jungle John himself. Toy heard people talking all the time about the world's record Jungle John was shattering. The rules were simple. Stay on the Ferris wheel for the full run of the county fair, the whole 38 days and break the previous record by nearly a week. He was allowed off the ride for fifteen minutes every eight hours to hit the bathroom. Otherwise he ate and he slept on the ride. Round and round and round. His team from the station brought him hamburgers and pretzels from the fair, or fried chicken. And plenty of Pepsi. To communicate with his team he began sending notes in the empty bottles to order meals. Sometimes he passed them jokes written on little notes stuffed into the bottles that were read on the air because he wasn't broadcasting from the gondola. There were rumours he tossed a few refilled bottles out of the gondola, glistening yellow projectiles arcing through the air like a boulder from a medieval catapult. No one ever saw him do it. It was just one of those stories. In fact, no one ever saw him at all. He was hidden away like a relic waiting to emerge on the final triumphant day. So he simply existed on the Ferris wheel, perpetually on the move and getting back to where he started hundreds of times a day. No one knew what it was like in there for Jungle John. He was a living question. Would he last the entire time? Was he green around the gills the whole time? Would he just surrender, maybe bounding away from the ride on one of his bathroom stops. But he had stuck through with it in the end, wobbly getting off the ride finally to a small crowd of lukewarm applause. Had it been the same for Gagarin the moment the hatch was broken open and he was pulled from his module. Toy could not stop thinking about Jungle John.

Everything had changed in the instant after the water came. Life in the gondola quickly developed a new set of routines. Maybe like the routine that Jungle John lived with for nearly the number of days that Noah rode the ark. Like Noah, Toy had his provisions to take care of. He stacked sea salt flavoured popcorn, licorice and a vast number of Kinder Eggs in neat piles on the padded seat across from the one where he slept. He had hauled in so many Kinder Eggs that he planned to crack one open every morning after trying his luck catching whatever floated by in the water. He slowly unwrapped the foil, smoothing it out flat in case he needed it for something later. Then he carefully separated the two halves of the chocolate egg and before eating, pried open the plastic yellow core. He invented a ritual out of opening the egg where he'd try to put together the Kinder prize while nibbling bits of the chocolaty shell so that both were finished at exactly the same time. The additive and the subtractive working up to a zero sum. He thought it might take a while to perfect the timing so that he finished building the toy prize at exactly the same time as he consumed the chocolatey shell entirely. There were plenty of eggs to practice on. A rare occurrence in the olden days could land a Kinder egg in his palm because Momndad did not approve of junk. He used to fantasize about collecting every Kinder prize there was over a lifetime, not knowing if it was an impossible mission. With a frown he looked over at the impressive pile of Kinder Eggs beside the other neatly stacked treat bags and he realized that in the near future he was going to be overrun with tiny plastic toys hatched from the chocolate ovals. His worry over growing the collection of Kinder prizes was caught up with the idea that he continually needed to find more things to eat. Despite all of the prizes he could assemble, he knew from past experience that there were very few doubles. He wanted to test out that idea and so he broke his first rule immediately. Instead of eating only one egg he ate five. Each time he opened a new one he told himself it was only to see if the prize was the same as one he already had. It wasn't. He finished assembling a plastic car, a truck, a plane, and a boat. The last one was a rocketship. He kept them all in a yellowish plastic Tupper Ware container fished out of the water. Very quickly he could see that the gondola would start filling up with too many little plastic containers. Toy didn't want to throw them in the water with the rest of the plastic. He had Tupper Ware for that, too. Back home, Momndad sorted things in Tupper Ware in the kitchen all the time: lunch meat, cheese, fruit slices, and even batteries. They even had larger plastic containers for really big things like bed sheets and old clothes. Plastic for everything. Momndad used to talk about the old people who had special plastic coverings for their sofas and chairs to keep furniture clean. Sitting on a couch like that, he imagined, made a crinkling that sounded like the noise of wrestling open a bag of Carmel Corn.

The more Toy ate, even in a short period of time, the more plastic garbage he made. It started to fill a green Tuff Stuff bag. Maybe there was a way to tie all of these empty bottles together in a raft and sail away but he dismissed the idea as silly. Wanting to keep the bottles out of the ocean he tied the garbage bag to the outside of his gondola and it hung there reminding him of a coconut suspended from the tree. After a while in the sun it started to stink. He'd have to get rid of it. That's when he got the idea of visiting another gondola to use as a garbage dump. He'd have to crawl along the big spoke and climb up one level to reach the red gondola. It wasn't too high, not much more than his own. Number 15-B was designated the garbage scow. The doors to that one were already open. No telling where the riders went. Navigating the spokes got easier with a little practice as long as he wasn't climbing super high to the very top. And reaching the top of the Ferris wheel was not something Toy saw himself doing. Ever. Going horizontally or sliding down to the water was as much as he could muster.

He had a garbage bag full of the Tupper Ware containers

and other things he didn't want slung over his shoulder. Empty garbage bags floated everywhere and were easy to fish. As he got closer to 15-B he saw a strange sight. A bird's nest was built on the top. As he got even closer he became more curious and a little more apprehensive. What if there was a bird inside that would jump out and peck at him until he fell into the water? Inching closer he could see the nest had no bird sitting in it so his courage and curiosity got the better of him. And so did the boredom building up in him in his tree house gondola with nothing much to do. At least this was a change of pace. Still, he needed to get up the nerve to climb right up to the nest. He'd never been this close to one before so when he got close enough to touch it he felt a sinking feeling. What was he going to do if there were babies inside? He'd never come that close to a living animal before. He had no experience with wildlife at all. There was not even a pet cat at home. He cautiously peered over the edge of the nest, noting it was much larger than he expected. Made of twigs and plastic straws, the nest was a weave of two worlds. And, it wasn't empty after all. In the very middle were four tiny eggs. They were white with little brown flecks. Not robin's eggs like the ones he saw at school once when a nature guest came to visit from the rescue centre to talk about local birds and endangered species. Robins were disappearing across the country along with owls and some other birds he couldn't remember the names of.

Toy thought these nest-eggs looked a lot like the ones he had for breakfast except they were very much smaller. Less than half the size. The baby birds that would hatch out of those eggs would grow into adults with sharp beaks so Toy needed to decide quickly if he was going to steal one. It would be a nice alternative to beef jerky and popcorn and chocolate. He didn't want to admit it because candy was something he thought about a lot before the water rose. Chucking the big green garbage bag through the open door of the gondola, Toy reached into his back pocket for a small white plastic bag he kept for the small things he found floating in the water. It reminded him of the thin bags Momndad used for buying fruit at Food City when he sat in the shopping cart piled high with Wonder Bread, boxes of Count Chocula, and frozen pizzas around him. It was the same kind of shopping but without the checkout counter at the end. In this case, he had to work quickly but delicately to snatch the egg before the Mom*n*dad birds came back. With care he placed it in the thin plastic bag, which he then tied to his belt. He quickly climbed back to his own gondola.

Safely back in his own space, Toy needed to figure out how to eat this uncooked oval thing. In truth he hadn't thought that far ahead. There was nothing to cook it in and no way to make a fire. Anyway, he didn't have a frying pan. Metal sunk, plastic floated. He thought about cutting it open like a lunch egg but expected the contents would spill out in a gooey mess. Instead he unfolded the smallest blade on his pocket knife and poked a little hole in the small end of the egg. With that, he sucked out the insides like he saw Mom*n*dad do when painting Easter eggs. As he had guessed it was slimy and he wouldn't describe the taste as good. And at least it was small and so quickly consumed. It gave him a stomach ache but different from the one the candy did sometimes.

He chased the egg with a bag of Nibs, and then lay down on the bench in his gondola and gazed up through the open emergency hatch to where the nest was, for the balance of the day. Eventually a gull came along and disappeared into the nest. It didn't seem to notice that one of the eggs was missing. Could it count? Did it even care? The gull simply got on with it. A while later the same gull started flying away and coming back with more regularity. Toy imagined that in a few days that the eggs would hatch and then many more days after that he might see the first baby bird fly off. It would climb very slowly to the edge of the nest. Toy might only see its small head. And then it would disappear back into the nest. After a few tries it might finally show its little body on the edge of the nest and then in an instant be gone. In his daydream, Toy couldn't conjure what a first flight looked like so the bird just wasn't there anymore. It was simply there one moment and gone the next. Though he'd been anticipating the first flight, seeing it soaring around the Ferris wheel for Toy's enjoyment, he couldn't really make a guess as to what that first voyage would actually look like. He saw all sorts of birds fly but he didn't know what a first flight seemed like. Once the baby birds were grown, Toy wondered how long it would take for one of them to come back and lay more eggs. And where they went in the meantime with nothing but the Ferris wheel to land on he could not even guess. What land did they fly off to out there beyond his own imagination? Like the Momndad birds that flew off to find worms for their babies, Toy figured he'd have to seek out more food once the candy and popcorn ran out.

## The Castle

The fog that had rushed in with the water disappeared just as suddenly. No warning. One minute thick fog surrounded the Ferris wheel like a prison cell. So thick that for a while he could barely see down to the carpet of floating plastic. Then, nothing at all except the white fog, as though the world might be reinvented once it lifted. And when it finally did drift away the last retreating wisps revealed a desperately empty world except for one thing on the horizon. The castle. It's iconic outline almost black against the sky nearly brought the same joy he felt on the first day in the park. Seeing the castle, or at least the upper part emerging from the water, had little affect on Toy's blank expression. It seemed as distant as the mountains in the side mirror of their car. It may as well have been a medieval dream, a beacon from the past as obscure to Toy as a knight's routine. Swimming to it was no more realistic than the truthfulness of the bar-b-cue ribs and pie he ate at the Medieval Times restaurant. He was that kind of medieval expert due to having three birthdays in a row at the dinner show. But he knew a crenellated tower when he saw one, even one that was a false remnant of the Middle Ages lost inevitably to a bitter nature.

With the castle exposed to the full intensity of the sun Toy's curiosity grew. The view of it was best if he sat on the roof of his gondola and exposed for hours and hours to the blazing sun, Toy was enormously grateful for the captain's hat with the black plastic ears on it. Otherwise he'd have had heatstroke long ago, as Mom*n*dad used to say. When the hat was originally purchased for him, on the first day in the park, he was far less enthusiastic. It looked like a hat for a baby and it made him look idiotic. But the one saving grace was that it came from the souvenir shop in the castle. Despite nearly having a tantrum over the whole hat buying incident, he gave in so they could explore the rest of the castle. Toy was awed by the building as soon as he saw it, which was near the entrance gate to the park. It was the biggest thing around for miles and so it dominated the lesser souvenir shops. Toy watched a short movie about the construction of the castle at a little shop. He learned it was supposed to be a gleaming monument to creativity among a sea of souvenir stands. However, the architect conceded to inevitability by agreeing to locate a restaurant on the second floor. The icon needed a purpose. The epic scale of it dwarfed everything around except for the Ferris wheel, partners in stillness and perpetual motion.

A modern ruin half sunk in its own moat, the castle was an impressive piece of architecture. Its pointed tower rose out of the water like the Lady of the Lake offering up Excalibur. It appeared in the distance, a hand and sword of some submerged giant forever about to rise silently from the depths. A diver meeting the water in reverse. Sadly, a distance that Toy knew was too far for him to swim no matter the treasure it might hold. The longer he stared at it the greater the distance seemed to be. Even with the fog completely gone it was hard to judge the precise distance because there were no other reference points. There was only the Ferris wheel and the castle, two technologies circling each other in a contest ages apart. Two points of reference, quoting nothing, on an open sea. Neither an original; Ferris's true wheel dynamited in the first act of industrial aggression less than a decade into the twentieth and most destructive mechanical century. The typhoid fever that ended Ferris himself, already reduced to poverty at the hands of the lawcourts, was nothing short of the plague that cleansed the medieval castle made obsolete by weaponized alchemy. Black powder. Forerunner of the combustion engine.

The castle that Toy saw was as mysterious as its medieval antecedents. Like the king's feasts, he imagined hordes of food that filled the daily buffet just waiting to be eaten. Momndad had planned on taking him to the buffet that night, but the water arrived and ruined all their plans. Then as now he drooled over the dessert trays that he'd seen advertised on the in-room television and in the hotel elevators that showed strawberry tarts glistening with fluffy whipped cream. An imagined treasure trove of food locked away behind an infinite moat. Just the thought of crossing such a wide channel conjured the terrifying image Toy had of swim lessons. At the outdoor pool around the corner from his house, where the water was always ice cold even in summer, swim lessons were offered to prevent children from drowning. That same person must have thought up the idea to plant huge trees around the pool, shading it and lowering the water temperature. It was empty most of the time except for lessons that consisted of swimming lengths over and over again. For some reason they always started in the deep end. So kids just learning for the first time had to get into the water and crawl in along the tiled edge of the pool to the deep end. It was sink or swim, literally. "We haven't lost one yet." The trouble was that Toy didn't trust that anyone would see him sink, and so no one would know to jump in to aid his rescue. So he clung to the tiled edge of the pool while the other kids pushed off the wall and headed quickly for the opposite side. By the time Toy got up the courage to push off, the whole class had already reached the other side of the pool and were on their way back toward him. Doing a version of the dog paddle, Toy swam directly into the waves made by twenty other kids now swimming the return leg. He could barely hold his head above the raging water line. Swimming in a storm. The waves were all the worse because Toy hated putting his face in the water so it resulted in even more water splashing his face. The waves caused him a loss of momentum because he stopped kicking to wipe his eyes and face. That was clearly the moment he recalled his head went under the surface.

The panic he remembered feeling in the pool presented itself as the dread at leaving the relative safety of his pod moored in an endless moat. He stared at the castle in the inconceivable distance for so long he must have blanked out.

He came around to the little voice telling him to stay calm. Stay calm. Except the voice was coming out of his own mouth.

He was facing away from the castle, looking over at all of the food he had gathered from fishing. Neatly stacked in groups according to type and contents. Thankfully, Toy did not have to face the panic of getting wet. In addition to the other items in his pantry, he had now collected bags of Sour Cherry Balls, candy corn, chocolate covered peanut bars, and a mountain of Lay's potato chips. Dr. Shore, the family dentist, would have said that a diet of mostly sugar spelled eventual disaster. A modern medieval plague. In time it would make him sick. He couldn't guess how long it would take, but supposed sometime soon. He could easily imagine the exact illness because Mom*n*dad, who would rarely let him eat this stuff, said it would rot his stomach. A rotten stomach looking like a hollowed out Jack-o'-lantern a week after Halloween. An orange mess heaving in the sun. The closest things he had to fruit were the candy apples that he fished for, and those had already been eaten.

As the sun was setting, Toy gazed at the castle. "Where did the day go?" He felt sure there would be loads of food in the restaurant. The upper part of the building was pretty much untouched. But, it was an unrealistic dream since there was no way of getting there without swimming.

"I might as well fly".

The First Storm

A full moon glowed behind a pleated blanket of cloud. But, every star was hidden. Toy lay on his bench in the gondola looking up through the escape hatch that briefly framed the blurry white sphere. The previous night, all manner of constellations were out. Toy watched them for hours because every so often a star would shoot across the night sky. This was the closest thing he had to a television show and he watched like Mom*n*dad used to do until static was all that was left to broadcast. The static was a lot like the stars in the sky, he figured, except that from the Ferris wheel he could only see some of the nearest ones. There were so many stars not visible to Toy's eyes that if he could see them their density would look like the static on the television. Toy watched the stars so long they appeared to shift in concert, rotating as a mass around an imaginary hub. They weren't simply painted on the night sky as he once thought, but revolved around an imaginary black hole in the centre of the universe. At least the tiny part of the universe Toy could see. Laying on the bench of his gondola, he wished he could pick out special constellations but the geometry of the night sky was as foreign to his knowledge as the medieval castle was to his time. He could identify a star as a point of light in the sky but sorting them into categories was impossible. Naming them was unthinkable. So, instead he made his own stories out of his own stellar groupings. A fierce dragon with a long tail made up of five stars and a line of three others. It attacked a knight wielding a battle axe several stars away. It was a victor-less battle waged over millions of years.

In the cloudy night, with no stars to entertain, Toy sat motionless with his eyes unblinking. Staring. He wasn't sure if he was sleeping. He felt sort of awake, but also asleep. In his mind there was a storm on the dark horizon. A fantastic tornado. It spat lightning at the ocean's surface that glowed red with each hit. The storm moved closer as the lightning flashed brighter. A stunning white flash turned night into morning and with each blast he could clearly see below him that the water was suddenly gone. Replaced by empty fields of perfect grass. His bird's eye view of the ground was unobstructed by the gondola as if his body had transformed into the gondola itself. He could see nearly every blade. A deep guttural hum from his chest drowned out all other sound. The grass sped by underneath him and was soon replaced by the black asphalt of a parking lot. He mounted the concrete border of the parking lot as a bike would when popping it over the curb at high speed. As he sped high above the parked cars he crushed them one after the other. He could feel the weight of his own force. The crushed cars were followed by one hundred year old red brick two-story buildings. One after another they crumbled. Their flat black roofs were turned to sand, sand of the castles washed away by an endless crashing of waves on the beach. Toy could hear the waves pulling at the sand in his dream, sucking it all out to sea.

With eyes open wide and staring into space, the sound of waves rapidly became the clucking of a familiar sound in the amusement park; the deadman's pin. Under the rollercoaster, the metal hook that dragged along the track under the train of cars to prevent them from backsliding on the first summit made that distinct cluck. The roar of the coaster cars rocketing over the downward slope mixed with the sound of a violent rain storm, and finally overcome by the higher pitch of the riders' shrill screams. When his head cleared and the last scream drifted away he was left with a single thought. Rain.

Toy's light nylon jacket and matching brown pants were no match for a torrent of rain. His clothes were also little protection against the rapid shifts in the temperature from day to night. When the sun was high he saw shimmering heatwaves in the air. But when the moon was out he could see his own breath. He worried that if rain came at night he'd freeze. Unexpectedly, the night of the full moon brought wind instead of rain. A new category of storm like the ones he saw on the television and Momndad talked about in whispers that stopped abruptly when he walked into the room. Still, he had heard enough to sense the tension in their voices. It was a tension like the one he felt as the gondola rocked back and forth like a swing blowing in a steady breeze. Then just as he thought it was at its peak, the wind speed picked up even more intensity. The car rocked from side to side. Within minutes it sounded like a foghorn without end. Metal clanged as loose bits of Ferris wheel whipped around. It almost sounded musical. A low horn with a percussion of bells behind, and then a faint whistle of the wind shear against the wires that held the Ferris wheel to the ground. It was the highest pitched whistle he ever heard. The car bucked sideways and it seemed like the whole thing would fall into the sea. But the wheel was a warrior against the gusts. It built to an overwhelming music of the windstorm, almost soothing. And still he could not sleep.

The damp nighttime gave way to a crisp morning stillness much faster than Toy thought possible. He felt exhausted from sleeplessness. Below him the carpet had changed drastically. The open-air pantry of plastic bags of popcorn and candy floating in the water was replaced by all manner of useless debris, bits of wood, and a thick tarp. The debris appeared to have a circular orbit around the Ferris wheel so it made sense that new things would float past all the time. The tarp was really large like a massive piece of yellow and blue circus tent. It was soaked and cracked in places but remained in one big piece. Because it took up so much space, he fished for no food at all that day. Nothing edible floated past him, his short reach.

The tarp was pushed up against the lower legs of the Ferris wheel so Toy had no choice but to try to remove it. He began pulling it toward him, rolling it like a rug. When he was nearly done winding it all up he heard a knock. He listened carefully. He could hear the sloshing sound of the water hitting the gondola he was standing on, his feet only inches into the water. A tiny wave leapt at his feet. Then the knocking again. He could hear it clearly this time but saw nothing. The tarp was all rolled up and out of the water. And then half a minute later, knock-knock. He looked all around and saw nothing. He forced himself to ignore the knocking. Focusing on his task, he tied a long length of rope to the rolled up tarp meaning to pull it out of the water like a massive hotdog. He climbed back up with the rope in his hand and then pull the obese wiener-shaped tarp fully up out of the water.

The tarp dried in the sun incredibly quickly, once Toy managed to unwind it and hang the material from its top two corners. It waved gently as laundry stiffening on a line in the sun. Using his pocket knife all day long to cut the tarp into four foot square sections Toy attached them to the outside of the gondola. He weaved some of the rope through holes he made in the top edge of the tarp and interlaced it with the wire mesh of the open-air part of the gondola. The coverings were like curtains mysteriously hung on the outside, or better yet, like the old sheet they used to put over the cage of their budgie at night. He started to think of the gondola as his perch.

Almost immediately it got warmer inside, nearly pleasant. He rigged up some more rope that allowed the bottom corner of each side to be pulled up, as a tent flap, to bring air and light into the gondola during the day and lock it down at night to keep in the heat. In the new comfort of his perch Toy lay on the bench looking out of the triangular window he made for himself with the tarp. Within an hour it stormed a torrent of rain that came out of nowhere.

Dry inside his cage and perched on his padded metal bench, Toy dug into some jerky and peeked out from behind the tarp to watch the storm rage. Huge raindrops, driven sideways by an intense wind, pelted the Ferris wheel. It was steady, unlike the night before. So much rain at once that he had to shut the emergency hatch. It rained all day and as night came on, with the moon in the background, he watched the character of the rain change from whole sheets to intervals and then finally to a fine mist. It remained hot even during the night and the cage got hotter still. Toy wished for a refreshing breeze now that the wind had died down. It was nearly unbearable. The hotter the tarps made it in the gondola the more water he had to drink.

The next morning the refreshed sun tried to rouse Toy's bleary eyes. It was getting harder to focus without any sleep.

Finding something new in the water helped to draw him to attention. Instead of food he fished out a few blankets and large pieces of mesh, tighter than a volleyball net with the holes very close together. A canoe paddle and a long wooden pole. And more rope. The rain had stopped completely and as the sun settled in overhead an unbearable heat returned. Toy hung the blankets, including a blue baby blanket with the remains of a satin edge, from the spokes of the wheel. The variety of coloured blankets hanging from the Ferris wheel spokes brought to mind the flags at the United Nations headquarters. The air dried them in minutes to a brittle hardness in the noon heat, except for the baby blanket that was softer though stained. He brought them all inside the gondola and succeeded in making a pretty comfortable bed with several layers. The dirty baby blanket with traces of its powder blue past was reserved for the top layer.

Gone Fishing

The day after the storm Toy noticed another sudden change in the constellations of the carpet. Milky Way gaps as seen from afar began to appear so he could see in places into the first few inches of the dark green water. He expected fish. Instead, nothing. Maybe the whoppers were deeper down and so he took the long pole and stirred up the water wishing to view something rise to the surface. Not even a guppy. The green, warm water was a cosmos of emptiness save the grocery of refuse Toy fished from its surface. He stared at the carpet for a very long time without blinking until the water bottles were a mosaic of colour and shapes glued together by plastic straws, spoons, and mustard packages. The black ribbon seemed thicker. He fished out a handful of water bottles. Each time he reached in to remove a bottle the ribbon momentarily disappeared.

"It must he nothing or a trick of the light."

As he reached for a package of beef jerky he thought he saw something white and long, deep under the water. It was floating maybe five feet beneath the surface and at first he thought it might be a dolphin.

"I really did stir something up."

It was no trick. He shook his head because he supposed that would be impossible since he hadn't seen a single fish.

"What would a dolphin be doing here in an ocean seemingly empty of fish?"

Still, he'd love the chance to reach out and pet a dolphin; it was on his list but so had the Ferris wheel been.

"Look where that got me."

He leaned closer to water the better to catch sight of the alabaster shape slowly rising to the surface. As it rose Toy could make out the distinct shape of a large object, bigger than himself. It was entirely white and oval. That's why he thought of a dolphin except that it wasn't swimming, more like hovering. Just as he was asking himself what kind of fish hovers, it broke the surface and Toy could smell it's horrid flesh. Bloated. Rubbery. See-through, the way his fingers got when he stayed in the bathtub too long. Not shriveled like his fingers got, but white as though the skin could peel off. It was no dolphin.

The inflated body of a person floating on its stomach. Toy could see only the swollen back. It had no clothes and barely resembled a human except for the fat legs and fin-like arms. The round middle of it was so big Toy thought of a helium balloon. He imagined it might continue floating up out of the water, breaking the surface to rise into the sky and fly away. Like a lost kite trailed by its string. Instead, it simply bobbed stupidly on the surface. An underwater dirigible coming up for air. It bounced a few times, bumping into a broken plastic chair before it began to slowly turn over on its side. A fat old man struggling to turn over in bed without anyone to help. He stared at the rolls of fat around its middle. The sinister lipless grimace painted across some snow white face stretched so taut it seemed about to burst. A great sarcastic expression of agitation and accusation. It didn't really surprise Toy. He felt as though he'd seen it all before, probably in a Saturday afternoon horror show.

Toy stared at the blistered cheeks and into its black eyes. Eyes directed up into the sky as though they could see beyond the atmosphere to the stars waiting silently until sundown. Terrified eyes revealing nothing. In contrast with the white flesh, it wore a wristwatch with a black band. Toy became more curious than frightened. He reached out and peeled it off the fattened wrist and fastened it to his own. The second hand was still moving.

Toy knew that it wouldn't take long for the body to rot and stink in the summer heat. So, he pushed it away with the long pole as one would cast off a small boat. It floated away mixing with the rest of the carpet debris until it seemed to disappear under the hot surface from where it once came.

The next day Toy became aware of the sun as it was almost overhead. He couldn't remember seeing the sun rise. He had been laying wide awake since the start and so lost track of whether or not he had ever been asleep. His eyes were dry and probably red.

He was feeling exhausted, the way he used to pretend to be when he wanted to avoid school. While he lay there in the morning under the blankets, he would try to make sense out of the whispers he heard coming from Momndad in the kitchen below his room. Stories about the insurance company where they worked going out of business and then about leaving their house. Toy pretended not to hear anything about those whispers because he didn't want to move and he figured that his silence on the subject might prevent it from happening. If he said nothing maybe things would just stay the same as always. Keeping secrets was easy if you stayed quiet.

After all, he never told them about the racoons he invited into the backyard by feeding them his left over dinner scraps. One of Toy's first memories in the house where he was born was leaving after-dinner scraps for a racoon. He'd seen it wandering around the backyard under the old oak tree, sad and homeless. Toy felt compelled to help the racoon when it looked up and they locked eyes. By morning the food was all gone. Toy felt supremely satisfied that he was the self-appointed neighborhood wildlife ranger. But the next evening under the tree not one but six racoons jostled against each other like they were killing time before their reservation at Mama Leone's Italian restaurant. How they silently communicated was a mystery, but it was clearly the same form of secret messages used by the five bodies that floated up to the Ferris wheel the day after Toy's first encounter. Bobbing closer and demanding to be recognized the dead floated nearer. The difference was that these ones were clothed. The leader wore a dark business suit with a red tie, its mostly bald head trailed long wispy hairs. As it came near, Toy reached out to grab hold of the coat. He felt it's obesity and pulling it close to him caused the body to wheeze. Water gurgled out of its mouth like a plastic toy he used in the bath. Toy felt inside the pockets of the coat and came away with a variety of coins. He put the change in his pocket instinctively.

Coins fascinated Toy. He examined the front and back closely, seeing as he didn't have any books. Not even a piece of paper to write on or he would have sent a message in a bottle long ago.

A coin. Wasn't it strange that only one side could be seen at a time. Heads or tails. He practiced flipping it for most of the day. Though he lost count he guessed that heads came up about half of the time. The surprising thing wasn't the number of times heads came up, but that there could only be one result at a time. A head or a tail. One or the other, not both. There was no compromise between a head and a tail. Coins also combined numbers and letters alongside miniature heads of people and animals.

In addition to the money. Toy became a collector of wrist-watches. Several of the bodies had expensive looking ones. After Toy riffled through their pockets he launched the floating bodies away from the Ferris wheel never to be seen again. Some mornings the catch was less, but almost every time his fishing pulled in at least some change. Nickels and quarters, mostly. Once he found a half dollar. It felt a lot like the Pull-a-String game at the amusement park, which always turned up a prize no matter how small. In this case, there was no trading up for a larger prize. He just kept what he found. After a while Toy had a nice collection of small change. The latest haul also resulted in a new coat, warm once it was dried in the sun. More like a leather bomber jacket with a fur collar. The inside was once white fleece and matched with his captain's hat so Toy felt like a test pilot. The gondola, his aircraft. He daydreamed about flying off into the thick grey clouds that hovered overhead, disappearing to a place he couldn't foresee.

Gazing so long at the clouds he lost track of time. Clouds entertained him with their perpetual shifting shape. Unlike the seriousness of the timeless stars, clouds entertained with their rapidly changing story. He was startled out of his trance by an alarm on the wristwatch going off at twenty-two minutes after five. The beeping alarm cut into the stillness of the clouds. The problem wasn't that he was surprised, though he did hate surprises, it was that all of the watches he had went off at the exact same time.

The Swan

Climbing up and down to the water strengthened Toy's grip and gave him the confidence to explore some of the other gondolas. A few were open, but mostly he climbed in through their emergency hatches. All of them had one thing in common. They were all completely empty. It confirmed that he was the sole resident of the Ferris wheel. But he wasn't completely alone. Seagulls' nests began to pop up on top of many of the gondolas, which he thought might eventually increase the breakfast menu. The trouble was that the proliferation of nests also drew crows. And that meant one thing. Competition. Toy spent more and more time chasing away the relentless crows, waving the paddle at them and clanging it against the metal spokes to scare them off. They got used to him pretty quickly so it became a mad race to the nest to gather a precious egg. He had help from the seagulls who were pretty good at scaring away the smaller predators. It was a joint effort but he was no honorary gull. While the Momndad gulls were out in search of some faraway food for their babies, he minded the nests against the black filchers. Did they know what he was really after? It didn't take long for the eggs to stop tasting like garbage and more like fish but it could have just been acquiring a taste.

On one of those trips, he was returning from one of the outer gondolas and he happened to look down at the water. Normally, he tried very hard not to look because it made him dizzy. But something on the surface caught his eye. Something large and white. He could hardly believe his eyes and contain his excitement. Below him, floating near the spokes of the Ferris wheel was a large fiberglass swan. Toy knew immediately it must have broken away from the ride in Kiddieland. One of his favourites.

"Where did you come from?."

The swan bobbed playfully as though it were nodding its head and inviting Toy to climb aboard. Toy quickly climbed down with his paddle in hand. The swan's mouth held a ring that was attached to a long rope hanging loosely down, trailing in the water. It was too far away for Toy to reach without getting into the water himself. So, he went back to his perch to retrieve the pole and climbed back down to the water quickly, before it could float completely out of his reach. He landed on the roof of the submerged gondola ready to reel in the swan. The wind had turned it around with the back end facing Toy, a ship sailing out of the harbor for some unknown place. It was almost out of Toy's reach. He should have tried to get it with the paddle when he had the chance. "I need that swan", he grunted as he stretched out with the pole to grab ahold and pull it in. His reach was coming up short. Angry with himself for wasting so much time. He grabbed onto the furthest spoke of the Ferris wheel with his free hand and stretched way out with the pole. The double knocking sound suddenly returned. He leaned so far out, balancing on the submerged roof that he could see inside the underwater gondola. Out of the corner of his eye he caught a glimpse of something moving inside. The distraction caused him to shift his weight and he began to slip. He could feel himself falling and as he fell, getting closer to the water's surface, the head of a body trapped inside the gondola threw itself at him. It banged hard into the wire mesh. Half jumping half falling, Toy landed inside the swan on his back with his feet up in the air. He hit his head on the floor and lay there stunned. As he blanked out, all he could think of was that angry face inside the watery gondola. Bashing its head against the door trying to get out, propelled by the power of the waves.

The next thing Toy knew the alarm on his watch went off at exactly twenty-two minutes after five. His eyes were already wide open except he couldn't recall how he got into the swan.

"Thanks for nothing. I don't need a call in the middle of the day."

He sat up in the swan and looked back toward the Ferris wheel. The current was pulling him away and he felt a cold sweat roll down his tense back. The swan had drifted a few feet from the base of the Ferris wheel. Toy tried to stand up and felt unsteady. It wasn't his head but instead the bounciness of the swan. He quickly sat back down. Looking at his feet with his hands around his face, there was the paddle. He was no boat expert, actually he had never been to summer camp or ever paddled a canoe. But he'd seen people do it on television so he started to splash the wooden paddle against the current. They started to go in a circle until he realized that he had to get up near the swan's neck and make a few strokes on one side and then some on the other. The strokes had to be balanced to get anywhere at all. Eventually he made it back to the Ferris wheel, exhausted. He tied up the swan with a bunch of knots so it wouldn't drift away again.

Eating and thinking for the rest of the day, Toy reassessed his whole situation. Having the swan was like getting a car for high school graduation six years early. He felt like he could go anywhere now, but the big question was where. The world suddenly seemed a whole lot bigger now. He and the swan were going to do great things together. "Where are the rest of your friends? How did you get separated from them?" Toy wondered if it was lonesome. In the fullness of the day Toy's last thought was that the swan needed a name. The coolest rides had the best names, like The Flyer which was the fastest wooden rollercoaster ever built. The swan deserved a name he could trust.

"Cyril. I'll call you Cyril, after my grandfather. He was in the coast guard. And you, my friend, are my rescue."

That night, Cyril bobbed in the water beside the Ferris wheel as Toy tried to sleep. Every so often the rope that bound Cyril to Toy pulled taut though it was truly their mutual gaze that bound each to the other. There was an immediate attraction that rendered the rope unnecessary. Toy immediately knew Cyril would never abandon him. The need was even greater when Toy closed his eyes and heard, or rather re-heard, the screams from the rollercoaster. He gave up trying to fall asleep and just lay on his back looking up at the stars. The sounds of the coaster were gone but the images lingered in silence. Momndad were standing in front of the Ferris wheel arm in arm. A tourist photo. They turned arm in arm and walked toward the castle in the distance. That was where he needed to go. In his gut, Momndad were waiting there for him. And the fresh fruit he had been dreaming of, too. Once in a while he took his eyes off the stars and turned on his side to check that Cyril was still there.

When the burning sun rose, the castle appeared to be not so far away that Cyril couldn't get him there in the better part of a day. Toy jumped in with the paddle and untied the rope. The swirling current started to take them in the castle's direction so it looked like paddling was going to be easier than he thought. The carpet was so big that Cyril bumped into debris and water bottles virtually all the way to the castle. While the sun was still high they reached the outer edge of the half-submerged palace. It sat in ruins looking more like a besieged medieval fortress. Most of the second story windows were knocked out by the wind and only the upper part of the main entrance to the building was free from the water. With just enough room to navigate under the portcullis entrance Cyril got inside. The whole place was eerily silent, like a cave filled with water. Some cushions and lots of stuffed animals floated around inside the huge cavity. The walls were decorated with shields but they were far too high up on the wall to reach even with the paddle. Getting up close to the wall Toy noticed that the paint was peeling off to reveal that the castle was not made of stone. The walls were plaster and attached to a thin metal carcass underneath. In places, the paper and plaster wall were coming apart and so he could see right inside to the skeleton structure. He scanned the large water-filled foyer space he was in but there was no staircase to the upper floor. Off in the corner he saw that so much of the plaster had come away that it was possible to climb up to the second floor if he squeezed through a small hole in the ceiling. He tied Cyril to the exposed metal piping in the corner and started to climb. He took the paddle with him to pry open the hole in the ceiling a little wider. That turned out to be a mistake when he was showered with plaster debris that got in his face and covered his hat. Recovering, he pushed at the hole with the paddle and managed to push his upper body through the hole to see into the dark restaurant.

After a few seconds his eyes adjusted to the dim light and he pulled himself through the hole. He was shocked by what he saw. The restaurant was in perfect condition. Or nearly perfect. Some of the tables were even still set for a meal, while others had half-eaten food left on plates nobody had cleared. People must have run off suddenly. There was no one in the whole place. Not a single body. Definitely no Momndad. The food on the tables was pretty much rotten. The smell of something wet filled the restaurant, like the stink of the pool changeroom. Toy made his way toward the kitchen. It was equally deserted. He ignored the rotten food in mid preparation and went straight for the freezer and the stock-room. The door was closed but not locked so he pulled on the large metal handle and pried the door open. It groaned as it swung halfway, stopping when the bottom edge of the door scraped to a stop against the floor. Barely open halfway, the tiny space it created was just enough for Toy to squeeze through. Once inside he found large cardboard boxes of liquid eggs, unfrozen burgers and chicken strips and melting fries. All of it was spoilt. Nacho chips and jars of salsa were all he could salvage that was still edible. "No fresh fruit." He grabbed a plastic bag and filled it, adding as many bags of salsa that would fit. Trying to squeeze his way back out of the freezer through the narrow opening the full bag got stuck and Toy had to gingerly coax it through without it tearing. "Why is the door not opening all the way?" It didn't make any sense. Taking in a deep breath he managed to make it through unscathed, bag and all.

The bag was hard to pull because of the heavy salsa jars. Dragging his loot along the restaurant's tiled surface was easier because of the slanted floor. Toy didn't recall such a steep angle when he came in through the hole in the floor. It was so tilted that he felt like he was walking through the crooked room in the funhouse. To maintain his footing he had to keep an eye on every step. That's when he noticed the strawberry sauce splattered all over the restaurant's floor. Like someone had carelessly dumped one of those big containers of dessert sauce he saw in the freezer. It dribbled in places and pooled in others. A poor imitation of Morse Code eventually abandoned for one large dot. As he stepped up to the puddle he realized it wasn't strawberry sauce at all.

Out of the corner of his eye he saw what might be a large person, just standing in the doorway. Toy thought the man was dressed in a cook's long white apron that looked small because he was so tall. The giant's head nearly touched the doorframe. What struck Toy, though, was the white apron splattered with strawberry sauce. It was a double shock. Toy was about to say, "what are you doing here?" He caught himself just in time. Instead, he backed away slowly in the way of discovering an angry dog is not on a leash. It wasn't strawberry sauce. Running was Toy's first response and as he turned to sprint away he checked over his shoulder to see if he was being chased. The doorway was empty. He expected the cook to come at him from the side but Toy's eyes narrowed so much he could only see directly in front of him. He wished he could disappear because he suddenly felt completely exposed in the middle of the large dining hall. Maybe if the cook didn't see him, Toy could sneak away quietly. In the silence, the alarm on his watch went off, again. Twenty-two minutes after five.

"Now? Really?" He was sure he hadn't said that out loud. Run. Run, was all he could think. Dragging the bag of food behind him he got to the hole he had made in the floor. He tried to push the groceries but the bag was too big. Toy hurriedly ripped it open and stuffed a few cans of salsa in his coat pockets and inside the lining of the jacket in the manner of a panicked shoplifter. Crouching over the garbage bag of food he looked up to see if the cook was coming. No one was there and that made Toy feel even more terrified because it would have been so much worse if the man jumped out at him. At least Toy wanted to be able to see him coming.

"Is he even there?" He didn't want to stick around to find out.

Toy squeezed through the hole in the floor and fell into the swan. Paddling madly, all he could think of was to get away as fast as possible. In his mind's eye he could still see the cook dressed as a butcher and holding a meat cleaver. And red splatters every-where. Had the man really been standing there silently in the cor-ner of the room? Maybe Toy just imagined it. It had happened so fast that Toy couldn't really be sure. He wasn't willing to stick around to find out for sure.

"Go, Cyril go".

The castle looked different when he got outside. The tower and spire were tilted wildly now. He was paddling madly and splashing toward the Ferris wheel but the wind was also picking up, pushing Cyril off course. Toy had to paddle hard to the cor-rect his course. Behind him, the castle let out a humungous groan as the tower twisted and collapsed under its own weight. It was made of nothing more than some drywall and flimsy metal so when the wind really picked up the whole thing fell apart, splash-ing into the water. Nothing was left behind to give anybody a clue it was even ever there, taking all the food with it. And the cook, too, he guessed.

Toy paddled toward the Ferris wheel rabidly but with a great deal of effort to stay on course. Otherwise he'd overshoot and then drift off to who knows where. His paddle stabbed so furi-ously at the water that Toy had to lean over and around Cyril's neck. They pushed into the wind but still moved quickly enough that Toy found himself exhausted and back in the gondola before he realized it. Catching his breath and consuming three bottles of water, he took stock of the new supplies and wondered how long they would last. Besides the few cans of salsa unaccompan-ied by chips, he would be back to the usual stuff pretty soon. That was when he realized there was no can opener. The only thing he could use to pry open the tin can was his little knife.

The remaining food source was the carpet. He continued to fish for pocket change and chose the best articles of clothing like shoes, green pants, a yellow coat, a blue sweater. Hanging them all on the spokes of the wheel to dry looked like the flags of many old nations or like the wings of tropical birds. The clothes whistled and flapped in the wind like the bids of his cage. How it looked from the horizon, he couldn't imagine. He stared at the horizon for a really long time until his mind stopped seeing. The lasting image was of the insane cook with the strawberry covered meat cleaver in his hand.

The Carpet

Watching the sun push itself out of the smooth watery horizon was a morning ritual. Each morning the day began with some thinking about Mom*n*dad because they had always opened the blinds in his room to wake him up. In those days the sun was already up by then so he never ever saw the sun rise. Breakfast with Mom*n*dad happened in front of the television, then the drive to school. Almost nobody talked. The sun was present but ignored. There was no drama of the sunrise in Toy's before days. So, when he looked out to the horizon he couldn't help but think of Mom*n*dad. He was convinced they were out there someplace and he imagined heroically paddling Cyril out to the horizon where they were waiting. So proud to see him. Smiling. And then he was hit with the reality of how far away that horizon was and how tiring the short distance to the castle had been. If he was going to see them again they'd have to find him. He waited in the same place like they told him. He'd wait. Something would happen if he waited. Toy was thinking these were daydreams mixing with the sleeping ones except that he was pretty sure he hadn't been asleep since the water had come.

On the morning after the castle, Toy thought he heard the exhilarated screams from the rollercoaster again. His eyes were already wide open when he realized the resounding shrills morphed into bleated cries. The imagined sounds repeated each morning like an alarm clock he didn't need because he was already up. In fact, he wasn't sure he'd actually fallen asleep. The most distinct sound came from the waves lapping against the legs of the Ferris wheel. Once he heard that and inhaled the odor of salt and brine the day was ready to start. But this morning the sound and smell was completely different.

As if he had been transported overnight to the moon, it was eerily static. The gondola wasn't rocking in the breeze. And he could have spent the night in a freezer, it was so cold. He could see his puffs of breath and his body shivered. He pulled two more blankets on and ducked under the covers. Putting on an extra coat and with sox for gloves, he emerged to an intense light coming from outside the gondola. The sky was turquoise and not a cloud about. The white light was coming from a frozen layer of bottles and jagged shards as though the water had solidified in seconds. He met Cyril, fully dressed for winter. The swan was cemented in place, looking sad and confused about its loss of mobility. The ice was so thick Toy couldn't see any water movement underneath. It was totally solid. He put a foot on it. Nothing. Kicked. Nope. Stomped. No. He stood on it with both feet and all he heard was the crunching sound of rubber soles on dry snow. Holding onto Ferris wheel beam X-33 with one hand he jumped up and down to see if the ice would crack. Definitely nothing. There were dozens of frozen water bottles and other plastic bags of food stuck permanently in the ice. Specimens in a stubborn collection.

Cyril looked at Toy pathetically, amidst a hardened carpet of fake plastic diamonds glinting in the bright sun. The glare hurt his eyes so he pulled the captain's hat lower over his face and looked out to the horizon. It looked like the jagged landscape of ice extended as far as he could see. He may as well really be on the moon or some icy comet speeding through space. A frozen sea of tranquility. He wondered if this meant he could just walk out. Escape on the solidified sea. This was his big chance. If he walked long enough in one direction he'd have to find something. But Momndad would want him to wait. So when he finally decided to venture out onto the ice it was no easy choice. Not because he was afraid to fall into the water – he was – but because he was moving away from his usual routine. And he liked routine. Cyril was part of his routine and he didn't want to give it up. His longing to know where Momndad were outweighed everything.

Cyril looked at Toy. "I know. I'm supposed to wait here for them to come to me. But I can't wait. I have to find them myself. You wait here. I promise that if I find them I will come back for you. I won't leave you behind no matter what."

He bundled up some food packets in a plastic bag that he

tied to the end of the long pole and strode off like a hobo. The sun was shining brightly through the crisp air. Within minutes he was getting hot in the double coat so he removed the outer layer and just left it behind after dragging it about twenty feet. He was starting to sweat even with one coat, which he unzipped. He wasn't tired. Just sweaty from the bright sun. Pretty soon he was feeling a little nauseous. As he walked he had the uncanny feeling of seeing himself from above and behind. Like he was a bird watching himself walking across the tundra. The horizon was getting no closer.

He had to take each step carefully to avoid the uneven parts of the ice. There was no path, just an endless expanse of patchy terrain shining brightly as if intentionally trying to blind him. The captain's hat was barely keeping the sun out of his eyes so he resorted to twisting his head to the left to compensate. With his gaze tilted, he had nothing on the horizon to aim towards and so he grew nervous about walking in circles. He was getting hotter and even though he already discarded some of the layers. A steady trickle of sweat idled down the middle of his back. He ignored it.

He was more focused on the fear of walking in circles. In movies the stranded always walked in circles. This was the very reason Momndad wanted him to stay in one place. Walking in circles literally would get him nowhere except more lost. Waiting for things to resolve themselves was their idea of a solution. Big problems always worked themselves out, like the problem of their car. They never gave up the old car even though the other families switched to electric. They kept on with the tradition of long rambling drives in the country on Sundays. Sometimes they wound up at the beach. Toy hated the beach. Not just because of the water. On one Sunday drive he remembered them talking about how catastrophe was always averted at the last minute. Something intervened. They were stuck in traffic while cars on the opposite side of the road proceeded past in an endless parade. The smoke coming from the tailpipes made Toy nervous. Where did that smoke go? He tried to count all of the cars parading past as though he could come up with some finite number, thinking

44

about how he could intervene. If it was only two hundred cars, he guessed it wouldn't be so bad. But he lost count at fifty. He remembered wondering why Mom*n*dad didn't seem to care. The endless line of cars made them feel normal and they liked things to stay the same. Repetition was at the root of their life. Every Sunday they went for the same drive in the country at the same time after lunch. Repetition and pattern. Perpetual order and the horrible beach.

He was walking towards the sun. But this had to be done delicately since the sun's arc might throw him off course. He wanted to keep going in a straight line, so he had to keep looking back from where he came to be sure of his aim. The Ferris wheel was getting smaller each time he looked over his shoulder and although it made him a little nervous to be so far away it was a sign of making progress. When not checking on his location he was looking down at his feet as he walked. Frozen water bottles, styrofoam cups, a toothbrush, and a catalogue of other plastic debris embedded in the ice. Away from the Ferris wheel he felt alone. Deeply remote. An ant trying to cross a desolate sea on the moon.

Step after step after step, making a percussive pattern as he walked on the frozen carpet Toy started to feel secure. The carpet even started to look like a wallpaper pattern. A water bottle motif alternating with mini mountain peaks of the fractured ice. Meanwhile the sweat continued to steadily drip down his back. Like the ticking of a clock.

He was focused on the ice below his feet when he heard the first snap break the silence around him. The kind you'd hear when a brittle tree branch was broken over your knee. The kind of branch that bent ridiculously before snapping and backfiring in your face. He avoided snapping branches. Then, he heard another snap and a third. Except there was not a tree in sight. The last snap came from behind him, he was sure. So he turned around and in the distance saw the Ferris wheel looking as tiny as a Christmas ornament.

Every muffled and carefully planned step seemed so incredibly stupid all of a sudden. A shiver ran up his spine and he really felt alone, standing out in the open, suspended on thinning ice over who knows how much ocean. Unfreezing. And who knew how rapidly. Toy immediately started back to the Ferris wheel. Was it a mile away? Or more? Faster, breaking into a run. The icy air burned his lungs and stuck in his nostrils but the hot sun beat down. As he ran, taking lumbering strides both wild and uncontrolled, the cracking got louder. More frequent. They were coming from everywhere, beside him and from a distance, so that it sounded like the percussion of an alien orchestra.

Halfway to the Ferris wheel the ice cracked and began to move. Violently. Large jagged pieces shot up in tree-trunk formations. Toy dodged and bumped into them alternately as he ran. Snap turned to bang. He heard the explosive percussion of ice bombs going off behind him, he guessed from behind because he saw nothing of it in his field of vision. He kept his eyes on the Ferris wheel but it stubbornly resisted growing larger despite the effort he expelled to reach it. Aching legs. Running in slow motion. It was a real life re-enactment of the night terrors he had when he was little, running from an unseen but impending danger. Taking steps but getting nowhere. The explosions, the ice chunks, and his legs choreographed in slow motion to his pounding pulse and agonized, wheezing breathes.

His senses heightened, as if caught in a lie. The absolute clarity of being caught with no way out. Running and fixated on the Ferris wheel, hoping it might save him. Sprinting back to the perch and Cyril, punctuated by a fear of everything around him. The sun fumed in a powdery blue and cloudless sky but the moon, out in daylight, distracted Toy's attention as he ran. Two competing celestial bodies in the same sky. The translucent silence of the moon, carved on the surface and washed out by the intense daylight increased his focus until it was the only impossible thing hanging above. A half-truth of a full moon. He ran along on the sharp hills and valleys of a moon punctured by ice detonations.

Fixated with the day moon, he pushed on and on. Toy

wished to be up there in its half gravity, bounding in huge leaps twelve feet at a time that would get him to safety in minutes. The astronauts on the moon had moved in slow motion too, but they covered more ground. Instead, Toy pushed ahead dragging his feet in exhaustion. Afraid to stop. He stared hard at the moon so that he almost didn't notice Cyril nearing, looking at him helplessly stuck in the ice. Large sections of ice were breaking off and piling up at steep angles between him and the swan as they started to float apart. He leaped across cracks a foot wide between the ice floes which quickly grew wider. It was like he was running across a puzzle depicting the moon that he'd broken up in frustration without finishing. All of the pieces were white. He hated puzzles. With puzzles there was no control. You were at the mercy of the creator and Toy didn't trust someone to create a puzzle he could solve. Nearer the Ferris wheel the cracks were further apart than he could jump without landing in the water. It was an unsolvable problem, with little time to figure it out. He was still running.

He felt sick that he might have run all this way just to get stranded on an ice floe that was drifting away from the Ferris wheel and out to sea. The car-sized ice sections started banging into one another like the bumper car traffic jam at the park. He'd been frustrated by those traffic jams before, and instead of just sitting there waiting for the attendants to fix things, he bailed. He simply stood up amidst the cacophonic noise of screams from neighboring rides and the competing music and stepped onto the hood of the next car. It wasn't moving anyway. The cars in the traffic jam were so close together he never needed to step onto the shiny metal floor, which he thought might electrocute him. He just walked across the hoods of the cars to Momndad and their shocked faces. They weren't happy but a lot less angry than the attendant who yelled at Toy until he was silenced by Momndad laughing so much louder. Looking to his left Toy saw Cyril waiting for him, straining against the long rope tied to the spoke of the Ferris wheel. He acted without thinking and leaped across the jagged ice floes like they were bumper car hoods. Less gracefully, he skipped across a couple of ice floes on his knees and then completely lost his balance on the last bump, falling backwards into the swan and hitting his head for the second time.

That was the last thing he remembered for a while.

The small waves returned not long afterwards. He was still in the swan. Toy patted Cyril's head and climbed wearily up to his perch. The usual meal was eaten while gazing suspiciously out to sea. He was back where he stated. All trace of the ice was gone. He could have convinced himself the whole adventure was a dream if his legs weren't so sore. He could not make sense of where the ice came from or where it went. Something in him wanted to deny it. It might have broken up and drifted off like the bottles of the carpet, except the bottles still lingered. Virtually as many as before and he had no way of knowing if these were new or old ones. What was clear was that he couldn't predict the suddenness of the storms any more than he could guess what was going to be in the pockets of the next body balloon floating to the surface.

Getting right back to fishing brought a haul of change added to the collection. He had quarters from all of the years between 1991 and 2019, except for 1995, 1999, and 2003. He had more than thirty from 2010. A busy year for the mint, he guessed. He also picked up more black and brown leather wallets. Wallets excited him the most because they broke up the monotony of the day. He had a process of wading through the contents of a wallet slowly for most of the day, picking through the pictures of family and the identification cards. Everyone had a driver's license, which he took to piling up on a seat beside his bags of popcorn. He had those organized by birthdate. Then, there were the smaller piles of work identification cards that he filed according to employee number. Credit cards were organized by issuing bank. And then the miscellaneous ones such as racquet club memberships, store loyalty cards, and waterlogged business cards. But the items he was most interested in were the photos. Each wallet contained several wallet sized school photos of children smiling broadly. Smiles that betrayed a complete ignorance of their limited future. Who were they smiling for? Robotically they smiled because the photographer requested it, his voice raised at the end.

Smile? Their smiling faces had slid into the wallet pouches as pro-jections into an uncertain and certainly dubious future.

Toy spent the day imagining who these people were and playing detective with their lives. So he invented a game by tak-ing the contents of a bunch of wallets and emptying the pictures and cards into a single big pile. Then he would search through the names and pictures to put them back in their families. In one wallet was Mr. Tim Kroyer who had three kids, Phillip and the twin girls Jessica and Emily. He kept several school photos of them over the years, adding the latest on top of the older ones. It took a while to figure out who was who from their faces as they aged. And then of course it suddenly stopped because they got no older. Toy guessed that Kroyer's kids were a weak spot and he was nostalgic for a past when they were babies. That was why he had so many more pictures of them when they were tiny. As his kids aged into adults there were fewer pictures. So Toy imagined that the kids grew up and moved away, leaving poor Mr. Kroyer to Saturday afternoon at his private golf club by himself. Mike Roberts, who lived on Mr. Kroyer's street, had a membership to Blockbuster but no kids. He was very proud of his Schnoodle and had one stamp to go on his coffee card. He walked Pietree the dog past the café every morning and grabbed a cup on way back, Toy mused. Sometimes Mike would run into a friend with news of the neighborhood. Most of the time he silently watched the parade of people.

Opening one last wallet, Toy unearthed a shock. He blinked. It was a recent picture of Toy with Momndad. He had to look at it more than once to be sure it was really him in the picture. Which of the bloated bodies it came from he couldn't recall but he was certain he didn't recognize anybody he knew. Toy quietly went back to organizing the pictures and wallets and change. The family photo was separated from the others into its own pile of one. After a while he saw that it was flipped face down.

Toy didn't recall turning the photo over. With so many empty water bottles scattered around in the gondola, not a sin-gle one of them producing the desired genie, it seemed natural to give one a purpose. Unscrewing an empty bottle, Toy rolled up the only precious photo he had and popped it inside. Screwing the cap back on tightly he simply looked at the three smiling captives, stuck inside a plastic prison they were oblivious to. He was about to throw it into the ocean when he froze.

The White Island

Toy despised jacks-in-the-box. Turning the little handle on the box had no bearing on when the clown popped out. There was never a pattern to predict it. Toy was startled every time. He hated to be caught off guard when there was no pattern to anything. The same agitation existed around popping corn even though gobbling it up was a supreme treat before it became the main course in every meal. Anticipating the first kernel to pop with its abrupt ping routinely took him by surprise. Within seconds, the staccato bursts of the kernels exploding caused some additional distress over the correct proportion of kernels to pot size. He worried that if too many kernels were poured into the cooking pot, the overpopulation of popped corn would overflow forcing the lid off. Exploding and burnt popcorn might litter the kitchen floor. Once, Momndad overheated the oil in the pot and less than fifteen minutes later the lid blew off in a raucous explosion. The lid left a dent in the ceiling and a burnt smell lingered for days.

The burning popcorn scent agitated Toy's state. He still wasn't sleeping so even the popcorn smell that permeated the gondola got on his nerves. It tricked him into thinking he was someplace else. He was back in the park with the rides and the crowd and the popcorn. He smelled the hot butter and heard the pinging of the corn popping. Disoriented, he sat up in the gondola and pulled aside the tarp. It was hailing. The sky was awash in blue ice pellets pinging off the roof of the metal shell. The echo inside it was ear-bursting. He was an ant trapped inside the drum of a wind-up monkey toy. Being inside the monkey's drum was so intense that every beat felt like it would pop Toy's eardrums.

The clattering rose and fell in small and large groupings. It was an all-out assault. Toy watched the hail through the small opening in the tarp, being careful about getting too close to the mesh. Errant ice pellets bounced into the gondola and he didn't want to be feel their sting. Most were tiny but a few were the size of some of the coins he'd collected. He watched them melt leaving the smallest trace behind on the metal floor. Then, evaporating to a point beyond remembrance. He concentrated on the melting for so long and so intently that he didn't notice the hail storm had stopped.

No wonder he was taken by surprise to see a massive white island float past his perch. It seemed impossible to have this huge white island sneak up on him, but it did. It appeared out of nowhere a football field away. Shaped like a pyramid, he guessed it was four storys. A floating islet. It was too far away to paddle to and besides even if he did manage to get there, it would be impossible to climb. Its surface was broken and chipped like sculptor's marble before the carving started so it picked up the sun's rays and augmented them many times over. Even from a distance it was impossible to look at it directly. The white island gleamed intensely in the sun, or rather reflected. It appeared to be set afire as if a massive magnifying glass using the power of the sun cut a path through the ocean.

"It's like a death ray, burning."

He was unable to even look at it, try as he might, for more than a few seconds at a time. The sharp light bursting from the island resembled the white blast of a lighthouse. A floating beacon yet insufficient as warning. Unable to see it clearly he couldn't track it, either.

"What do you mean, you think it's coming this way?", he yelled to Cyril. "We can't get away in time. I'm not ready to leave and I'm not packed up."

Toy was startled to think that the island might slam into the Ferris wheel. What concerned him the most was that it seemed to be moving slowly from a distance but he reasoned that up close it was going pretty fast. If it collided with the Ferris wheel there would be no contest.

It was a like a solitary celestial body looking for companions.

With his hand raised to ward off some of the brilliant light, Toy could see the island's trajectory. It had an orbit of its own obeying laws of a unique gravity. The island was too massive to be caught up in the rotating current of the carpet. It was stronger than the waves that swirled around the base of the Ferris wheel.

"It's coming closer but I think at an angle that might miss us. It's going to be really close." Cyril excitedly bobbed in protest.

"I know you're in the water and I'm up here. But it doesn't matter one way or the other because we're both sitting ducks."

The island crept closer. The bottom of the island scoured against the leg of the Ferris wheel and the gondola shivered in distress. If the impact had been head on, like Toy had feared, the wheel would surely have toppled. Instead, it was more of a glancing blow. Still it caused so much vibration that Toy felt it in his teeth. The grinding sound of two families of carbon abrading one another was like a poorly played tuba in the school band. The island was so close that Toy could see its etched surface. Striations and markings of an alien language. A language on an island seemingly transported lightyears from some Venturi or alternate universe. It had neither companions nor origins. Compassion nor malice. It was a celestial body brought to the surface of a watery planet and whose own isolation bore no equal. Alone. It dawned on Toy, from within the massive shadow it cast, that he was a lot like the island. Lost. Separated. In an unknown orbit. The shining surface of the white island reflected Toy's face back at him and he saw changes on his own surface. There was no mining its depths. There was no need.

Toy surmised that the island must be several times larger under the water, the hidden part bearing the real danger. What lay under Toy's own surface was as much a mystery as the state he fell into in the burning light once the shadow moved on.

Toy knew nothing of being in a state when he was in it. And the only indication of coming out of one was the sound of the delighted screams from the rollercoaster. He could feel the rumble of the rollercoaster cars deep inside his chest. It lingered for minutes after his eyes were fully open. It happened the same way each time. A repeated intro to a television program on perpetual syndication, of which the opening sequence was unhappily memorized. Black screen. The rumble of the rollercoaster followed by joyous screams turning rapidly into horrific screeches and then the sound of people scattering in all directions. A subtle change in pitch was all the difference. Open to seagulls circling overhead against a cerulean sky. The cry of gulls washes out the screams. The birds fly off all at once leaving silence. Three beats of silence. And then only the metallic creaking. And Toy remembers he's still on the Ferris wheel. Enchantment to panic in the span of an instant. It was the pitch of boys and girls confronted with something they hoped could be ignored. Hope was not the plan. Not even *a* plan. The screaming reached a frantic timbre and then the state ended. It took a few seconds for him to figure out he was actually awake.

Only the wristwatches provided any proof of lost time besides the obvious missing white island. The island had completely disappeared and Toy could not account for four hours. He was upset with himself that he had missed seeing the island move off toward the horizon, assuming that was where it went. The big bother was that Toy had to admit he was no longer able to be in control of himself at all times. It was like living with a jack-in-the box. He never knew when it was going to pop out. He hated the surprises.

## A Creature

Toy calmed down a bit when he returned to routine. His routine. He climbed down to fish and since he liked finding things in the pockets of whoever washed up he was content. Pattern was comfortable. The usual coins and cards. But oddly, the suit jacket on the first one had a sticky film on it that made the material unwearable. The second and third had the same. As he pulled on the fourth, lifting it partially out of the water Toy noticed more of the thin black ribbon floating in the water. He reached in to pull on the ribbon but it disintegrated in his hands and it coated his arms with something like molasses.

The departure of the white island revealed an object in the distance Toy hadn't noticed. Far off near the horizon. A small black mass silhouetted against the white sky, barely rising and falling with the beat of the ocean. He kept an eye on it for a long time and it didn't move. Just the rising and falling with the waves and so Toy made the only assumption possible. Something was out there spying. Why else would it stay in one place, almost but not quite out of Toy's sight. It meant he could be seen and all of a sudden every movement Toy made was self-conscious. Long ago, after a fight at school that landed him in the principal's office he told the truth to Momndad. The other boy looked at him in a way he didn't like. Toy needed his space, to read, to think, to breathe. The boy, Lawrence, invaded it. The fight started because he felt threatened when his classmate had locked onto Toy's eyes from across the room. The staring was like a knife so Toy went after him, leaping over the desks but missing his actual target. Knowing that he had uncorked an unstoppable force, Lawrence immediately ran to the pencil sharpener on the wall. He quickly cranked the handle around to produce a newly minted tip. As Toy caught up to Lawrence and was about to strike he felt a punch on the side of his head. Lawrence's pencil was still sticking out of Toy's left temple like half of a trick arrow sold at the joke store. The kids in the class screamed. The teacher nearly fainted. They both got sent to the principal's office, making up on the way. Mom*n*dad were called in to take Toy to the hospital where he got three stitches. Lawrence learned not to look at Toy in the eye.

It was no surprise when Toy became obsessed with the creature looking at him from a distance. If he squinted his eyes or gazed at it through the tiny hole he made with his fist - a flesh looking glass - Toy believed he could see its oblong body rise beyond the surf. Its huge back fin waved in the wind, and in fact it was that movement which convinced Toy he was looking at a dragon. What else had an elongated body and bat wings?

"I see you," he said coyly. It was hovering in one place because it was hurt, he surmised. It's a small wound, not critical.

"What do you mean, it won't harm me?" he asked Cyril critically, "How would you know?"

"We could head out there with the pole sharpened to a pencil-sharp tip. That's what we could do."

"Why not kill it? We had better hurry up while the creature was still injured or we don't stand a chance. The storm must have brought it down, trapping it in some of the ropes we found in the carpet. That's why it's struggling."

"We need to get going before it wriggles loose." Maybe it had even been damaged in the frozen ice, or dived down under to emerge once it melted.

"Maybe," for all Toy knew, "the dragon had been spying on us the whole time since the water rose."

Attack was his first choice. He certainly wasn't going to be chased out of the Ferris wheel. "This place is mine." He was sure this creature was coming for him as soon as it was able so it had to be dealt with it right away. Only how and when was the question. After all, a dragon was an unthinking beast that only understood killing. "Could be coming for us any minute." It made Toy feel incredibly uneasy. He cursed himself for wasting so much time already. He pictured himself trapping it in the netting he kept on the spokes to dry clothing. He saw himself stabbing at the writhing dragon, as it whipped its wings helplessly. About to deliver the final blow, Toy pictured it rising out of the steaming ocean.

Five times the size once in the air, it shook off the water like a hairy dog on the beach. Unhurt, all along. It turned its gaze in Toy's direction and took in a deep breath.

"What are you thinking?" Toy gasped to himself. Killing a dragon was a notable over-estimation of his abilities.

"Maybe I can scare it off like I did with the crows". The trouble was that crows always came back. They weren't really afraid of people, no matter what was thrown at them. And even though they should be afraid, because of what people could really do, they weren't. The more Toy thought about the dragon the more he felt sorry for it, trapped out there and struggling. Weighing his options, Toy finally decided to venture out to the dragon to see how badly it was injured and to see if there was a safe way to rescue it. In the stories he read, dragons could talk so maybe this one did too. Toy imagined himself cutting away the ropes that bound the dragon with his little knife. The grateful dragon would speak to Toy, thanking him. And he would offer a ride on its back and the pair would fly off and away from the Ferris wheel toward the unimaginable horizon. So invested with the dragon was Toy that he worried more about being too late to save it than being roasted alive. He needed to hurry to save the dragon, a dragon who would in turn save Toy.

Paddling out to the dragon with the late sun at his back seemed to Toy like the best plan. That was the only way to sneak up on a crow, which Toy had done before. The crow would let you get close if the sun was behind you because it was distracted by the brightness and couldn't quite make you out as a threat. Using this same tactic, the dragon would be blinded to Toy's coming until it was too late. Then Toy would heroically pull out his little blade and free it from the ropes.

Hopping into Cyril, Toy had to reassure the swan it was safe. On the paddle out Toy found he tired more quickly than expected. He was going against the wind. As he got closer he could see the dragon's black wing frantically beating against the water. It was rhythmically pounding the water's surface, trying to escape from the web-work of ropes holding its body on the water's surface.

The ocean swelled this far out and Toy failed to notice until he was really in it. By then it was too late and he had to concentrate on paddling Cyril without turning over. He only saw the churning water a few feet in front of the swan to avoid releasing the panic building up in his stomach. So much was his focus on the water that Cyril ran straight into the dragon like running aground on a desert island. It made a hollow echo similar to an empty oil drum. The hard skin of the dragon was covered in a webbing of ropes that Toy started immediately to cut away. As he did, the black tattered wing of the creature whipped in the wind, slapping at the roiling surface. The spray it kicked up made it almost impossible to see. For all he knew it was a downpour beyond the spray the dragon made in its immediate circle. He continued to cut away so frantically he nicked his finger. A tiny cut but the blood ran freely in the haze anyhow. He pressed his hand to the dragon's body but there was nothing. No heartbeat. At first Toy thought he was too late.

He pounded the body with his bleeding fist. A single hollow echo. Boum. He pounded again.

Boum. The spray was obscuring his sight. Toy felt completely hollow inside. Not because the dragon was dead before he got there. But on account of there being no dragon at all. What possessed Toy to paddle all this way out to kill a sailboat, a boat on its side with a massive hole in it the size of foolishness? He had come to uselessly rescue a broken sailboat. Half sunk in the waves, it's foresail whipping the wind. Toy cried. For the first time he cried in frustration. Not for the loss of some random idea of rescue and not for the loss of Momndad. But for the loss of the dragon he came to save. For nothing. For some waterlogged boat in place of a heroic quest.

Crying, he pounded on the hull again. Boum. In retaliation, the black sail whipped him sharply on the arm as though it were a wet towel. Snap. His despair switched to anger. A hatred of the boat far greater than the one he initially had of the dragon swelled up so suddenly he could think only of stabbing at the sail. He grabbed ahold of it as it readied for another swing in the wind and slashed at it with the knife. The blade tore a long gash in the sail and the tear rippled along the material splitting it nearly in two. The wind dipped into the sail and the force almost lifted Toy off the ground. He pulled against it like an errant kite.

At that moment the bifurcated sail brought forth a clear picture of escape in toy's mind. He acted quickly to tie Cyril to the boat's tackle. Climbing onto the half submerged hull he cut away at the sail until he came away with a large piece, hastily rolling it up. He thrust it into the swan. Untied and cast off, he paddled frantically away and back in the direction of the Ferris wheel.

Finally back at the perch and with his new black bundle under his arm, he tied up Cyril as the sun was hitting the ocean. Back in the gondola the bundle was shoved under the seat opposite his bed. He arrived just in time because the wind rose higher and whistled through the tarp. He struggled to close his eyes, unable to turn himself off. Eyes wide, the last thing he remembered was thinking that tomorrow was going to change everything. After that there was nothing.

**Wind**

The morning after the battle with the sailcloth, the wind was still and the water calm. A sheet of glass. Toy scumbled down to the water's edge to get a round of fishing in. The first few bodies he came across had nothing but empty wallets. But there were several bags of popcorn and Hot Rods so not a total loss.

The next body made Toy stop and stare in disbelief. He had seen this one before, the hideous one with the red tie. At first he wasn't going to bother with its pockets but changed his mind at the last moment. To his surprise he found change, lots of it. And another watch with a black band. Then he noticed the body surrounded by a larger black ribbon. A dark veil in the water. It left a trail that eventually feathered out to nothing though Toy had no time to think about its origins. His mind was distracted by the more immediate problem of the body. Particularly the contents of its pockets.

"I know I pushed it out to sea. I know I emptied its pockets. How did it come back?"

It was a mystery. And Toy hated mysteries. Puzzles the most. He loved patterns though. They were easy to find. But puzzles. Nope. In school, his teacher often read from the Encyclopedia Brown series of books. The title character, the Brown kid, was a twelve year old amateur sleuth who solved mysteries in his neighborhood. The kids in Toy's class were supposed to listen as the teacher read the story, like the one about the missing pet frogs, and suggest solutions to the problem. If you were listening carefully and could work out that someone in the story was lying or a piece of crucial information was missing, it was easy to guess who the culprit was. But, Toy could never figure any of it out so he stayed silent in the reading circle. In fact, he stopped paying attention altogether after the first page was read. That was always where Encyclopedia Brown lost him. Page One. Afraid to guess, he sat among the other kids hoping to avoid being asked a question so he wouldn't look as stupid as he felt. An imposter alone in his empty thoughts waiting for the story to end. The story he couldn't follow. That was the first time he entered a state. The tension in his little body evaporated suddenly through every pore, he grew very tired. Of course that was only until the next class exercise he couldn't accomplish, and then the whole cycle would start again. The present mystery was a job for Encyclopedia Brown.

"How did the body's empty pockets become full again?"

"What do you mean I'm mistaken? I know this is the exact one I saw before. And I emptied it's pockets. I can prove it."

"I know the balloons all look the same."

Maybe he was forgetting things. He had been having trouble lately keeping track of the number of food packages he had left. Some seemed to be disappearing. Or he was just losing count. He was sure that there had been seven small packages of CapnJack's Smoky Flavoured Beef Jerky, but now there were only five. Could he have miscounted? He had gotten pretty used to eating without really being hungry. "Stuff is definitely missing. And I know it can't be you."

There was really only one possible explanation. While in one of his states Toy was eating and who knows what else. The only other possibility was that there were pirates sneaking onto the gondola and taking away food but leaving Cyril alone. There was not a single clue to suggest pirates. If that was the case then he might even be having adventures while in one of these states. One thing was clear and that was that Toy needed to find some way of stopping them. The puzzle was impossible to solve without some information and the only thing he had to keep track of anything was the wristwatch. So he decided to keep track of the time between states to see if there was a pattern. As for the mystery of the pockets, that one would have to wait.

"None of this will matter if my plan works. We're going to sail right out of here. Today."

Toy set about tying the frayed corners of the sail to prevent them from running like stockings. Then he cut holes in the four corners and ran some rope through the holes. next, he tied the sail onto one of his poles and tied the pole under the chin of the swan, using its long neck as a mast. With the ropes tied to Cyril's tail, he thought it would be possible to sail into the wind. The final task was to tie the paddle to the tail as a rudder so that he could steer with one hand while the other worked the wind.

As the unbearable heat dropped just a little bit, he took Cyril for a short trial sail. It was a test drive to see if the contraption would work and to prove that he could steer the fiberglass craft. He took the Timex from his collection so he knew roughly how far he had gone. Pushing off from the Ferris wheel to avoid getting caught up in its spokes he let the rope go. It was a good thing too since Cyril took off the moment the small sail let out. With little weight holding it down, Cyril accelerated speedily. Up and down the waves the sail pulling at Cyril's neck threatening to snap it in two. Toy struggled for control and at that point one thing was absolutely clear. There was going to be no trial run. This was it. And of course he had left all of the food behind. It was like sending the first Russian into space only to tell him on the way up that mission control had decided at the last minute to send him all the way to the moon instead. Small course correction, comrade. Even he had brought a wristwatch. Aside from the Timex Toy had with him only the clothes he was wearing, his light jacket, and the white captain's hat with the missing black ear.

He was surprised to see how fast the boat could go. In minutes he was so far away that the Ferris wheel was gone from the horizon. Water was the only thing he could see in every direction. It was the feeling he had in the pool dog paddling more than an arm's reach away from the side. He was so anxious that his left leg started to bounce up and down. He didn't have a free hand to hold it down to make it stop.

"What if we get stranded out here, with no land in any direction? That's what you're worried about? I'm more worried about a wave tipping us over, buddy." He couldn't decide which was worse. Lost or drowned. He felt bad about scaring Cyril.

When they were gone exactly half an hour Toy noticed

something on the horizon that looked like it might actually be land. He grew extremely excited.

"See, I told you everything was going to work out fine. Why do you have to be so negative all the time? Really."

As they got closer it looked like a long thin island or a peninsula barely above the new sea level. Peppering the length of it, something glinted in the red sun like lights from a few dozen cottages on a distant lakeshore.

"Could it have been that easy? Was land this close the whole time?"

The excitement of what the peninsula might offer for food was difficult to contain. He steered in the direction of the thin landmass since it stretched so far across his field of view that avoiding it would have been almost impossible. Toy's mouth began watering at the prospect of the fruit that might be growing on the island, starved for anything sweet that wasn't packaged sugar.

As Cyril got closer, the wind died down considerably because the peninsula acted as a natural break. So weak was the wind in this place that he had to pull in the sail and paddle the rest of the way. As they got very close the wind was let out of Toy's sails, too.

"Yes, I can see it's not land."

Almost on top of it, he could not believe his eyes. There was nothing natural about the peninsula. Nothing, at all. Piled up on top of one another were a collection of cars, rusted and broken, twisted into a thousand configurations to form a metallic jetty. He could see that those on the surface were heaped on top of others submerged as far as ten feet below. A few of the upended cars on the surface were smoldering with mini fires like a crude campfire set by what he imagined were little mechanical men. Mirrors and chrome glinted in the sun.

His disappointment was intense.

"I guess there's not going to be any fruit."

The shallowness at the edge of the island would have been walkable except for the jagged metal concealed under the water.

The cars above the surface were equally sharp in places so climbing out of Cyril seemed impractical. Toy paddled along the pile of cars looking for anything of use. Finding nothing he tied Cyril to a grey pole jutting out of the water.

He wasn't alone. Perched on the tire of an upturned rusted Chrysler Impala, looming above him, no more than three feet away was a Great Blue Heron.

"What are you looking at? This isn't the complaint department."

Seeing the heron's grey body impossibly balanced on its spindly legs was almost laughable. But, there was nothing funny about its size. The heron was huge. It shocked Toy, who'd gotten used to the smaller birds flitting around the Ferris wheel. Nearly larger than Toy, the bird glared down its narrow beak as would a needle-nosed bespectacled professor. The massive bird met Toy's gaze in judgment. Toy waited for it to fly away, afraid. It stood there instead owning the tire, motionless.

It's expression didn't change. Toy stared back, daring it to do something. He had an urge to wave his arms wildly to scare it away. And stopped himself. For a moment it appeared blind, unable to sense Toy's presence. Or it was ignoring him. What might have been the cause was un-guessable. A flightless and enigmatic statue, it seemed, the sort used to scare away other birds. A plastic form, mass produced, meant to sit atop some neighbor's eaves. A menace to ward off the crow. Toy started to seriously doubt it was alive. It hadn't moved once. If it had the ability, Toy had no proof. It could just as easily be plastic. Real or plastic, those were the choices. There was nothing in between. He had a hard time guessing.

This exact thing had happened to him before. When Toy was much younger he was taken to Niagara Falls. Momndad were in awe of the tons of water that dropped every second over the fall's edge, chewed up in the raging rapids below. The little boat called the Maid of the Mist that tempted fate by delivering over-excited tourists to the churning mountain of water just beneath the falls, barely out of reach of disaster was deemed far too dangerous for little Toy. At least that was how Mom*n*dad said 'no'. Toy wasn't disappointed in missing the boat ride. There were plenty of terrors on dry land, over on Clifton Hill at the House of Frankenstein, for instance. Parked in front of Frankenstein's house was a 1928 Cadillac touring car, which seemed to have nothing whatsoever to do with haunted houses or any of the Frankenstein movies. But, sitting behind the wheel was the Wolfman wearing a blue suit and overcoat as if he were the driver of the invisible man, because the back seat was empty. The front windows were rolled all the way down, so a brave boy could climb up on the vintage auto's running board and reach his arm in all the way, and pet the werewolf's fur. At least that was Toy's plan. He'd been watching the werewolf for ten minutes and it hadn't moved an inch. It was clearly fake, like in the wax museum. Mom*n*dad said it was real and Toy, who didn't believe in werewolves, was sure it was fake and wanted to prove it. He hadn't realized that the kind of real Mom*n*dad meant actually referred to a guy dressed in a wolf costume. What was obvious to them was obscured in childhood to Toy. He was sure there was no such thing as a werewolf, despite what the movies said. So he climbed up on the running board and as he leaned his head very slowly in the window to get a close look, the creature's head turned sharply to face Toy's. Their eyes locked for just a second. Toy leaped backwards six feet like he was shot from a cannon. In front of the large heron, and with that fright etched into his brain, Toy was resolved. "I'm gonna find out if you're real. Last chance."

Toy rose up in Cyril as a challenge to the heron, but the little boat rocked unsteadily. Just as suddenly he sat back down. The Great Blue Heron reigned over the metal jetty. A plastic king for a rusted car island, thrust out of the ocean like tectonic plates had crashed together. Toy sat incredibly still in Cyril. Everything had already been decided, and Toy felt powerless.

"Say something!", he broke the heron's sanctimonious silence. "Whadya want? What?"

As he tried to balance the boat under his feet, the heron rapidly spread its massive wings. Caught by surprise, even though he had expected the bird to be real, Toy leaped backward falling and hitting Cyril's tail. Just like the time with the werewolf. He felt like an idiot. He just barely avoided falling into the water where broken and twisted metal lingered dangerously below the surface. He hit his head on the seat back, again. The last thing he remembered was the heron disappearing over the edge of the jetty of cars, cackling with laughter.

The Jetty

The sun was high overhead by the time Toy opened his eyes. It was the first time without the mixture of the shrill cries from the rollercoaster and the circling birds. On the jetty there was only the sound of the wind whistling through the cars, sucking out the moisture from the air. His mouth was so dry he could drink a whole case of water bottles. There was one in his jacket pocket and he polished it off in two gulps. There was no water left to conserve, being so far away from the carpet he had come to lean so heavily upon.

"Where will I get more?" It was the first time he thought about how weird it was to be hunting for water in the middle of an undrinkable ocean. An ocean cleaved in two, he had just learned, by the sharp edge of the metal jetty. Toy felt that he was lost in the middle of a man-made ocean. For the first time, away from the Ferris wheel, he felt as though he were adrift and without a clear purpose. He imagined what the scene would look like from orbit. An insect crawling along the edge of a straight razor. The jetty extended as far as he could see in both directions, which meant he had no confidence to round it in Cyril. The first astronauts on the moon must have felt trapped in the same way. Not so much because they were two hundred and eighty thousand miles away from earth and living out of a tin can the size of closet, but since they had traveled all that way only to be limited to the distance they were allowed to venture from the landing module. As true explorers they must have wanted to walk toward the horizon, freely in any direction. Surely, it wasn't allowed. Houston had the astronauts on a long, long invisible leash. Toy wondered if they felt treated like twelve year olds. And he felt the same way he imagined they did except there was no one holding him back. There was no Mission Control of the Ferris wheel.

The jetty was as barren as the sea except for its lone occupant, the heron. And even it had deserted the metal breakwater. When it flew off over the far side all that Toy remembered was the cackling laugh. The burst of squawks from the its long beak lingered long after the great bird was out of view. Toy wanted to follow after the heron. He figured that it knew something he didn't.

"It must be headed toward land only he can see."

And People. Momndad. "They could be close, maybe just on the other side of these cars. They're waiting. I can't give up and just go back to the Ferris wheel without checking. They might wait forever."

He pictured them wondering what happened to him. Lost without him.

To learn what was on the far side of the jetty he was going to have to leave Cyril, even if only for a little while. But he was reluctant and worried. The last time that he had been separated from something that mattered to him had cost Toy his red three-speed bike. He had locked it to a post at the mall, and when he returned to go home the lock was sitting there by itself, uselessly. Someone had taken the trouble to pick the lock, steal the bike and secure the lock to the post again. At first he thought it had been a joke. And so he looked around to see who might jump out from behind a fence with his three-speed, laughing. There were plenty of kids who would do that. And Toy would have had to laugh too even though it wasn't funny, just to get his bike back. Even though he was upset fighting never worked against bigger kids. But, no one showed up at all. Toy's expression turned quickly to despair as the terror of losing his one and only bike sunk in. His walk home was bad, not so much because he anticipated telling Momndad but because he had been so attached to the bike. It went everywhere with him for three summers and now it was in someone else's hands. He imagined some older kids from down the street taking the bike apart for spare parts. He felt helpless not being able to protect the bike the way he wanted to. They were inseparable partners on errands to pick up milk or in joyriding around the neighborhood. Toy washed it every week, like the next door neighbor did his car on Sunday. Next summer he planned to be big enough to try riding with no hands like some of the older ones. Those kids all had 10-speeds but Toy loved his small three-speed so much that he pictured riding it his whole life. And so it was torture to him to think that he couldn't find it.

The bike was his responsibility and he had hadn't properly taken care of it. It didn't matter that he had locked it up, because he had to admit that he had barely twisted the dial on the lock. He always left the lock in an easy to open position so he could ride away quickly and now his laziness was the cause of the bike being taken. He wasn't going to tell Mom*n*dad that part. He was going to explain it was like a kidnapping without a ransom note. For that reason he knew instinctively he was never going to see that bike again. So, leaving Cyril tied up to a car, bobbing in the waves, felt nervously familiar.

The other unsettling thing was that he was going to have to climb the pile of sharp metal cars to get to the other side.

Examining the jetty closely, he tried to pick a route up the cliff of cars. A junkyard wall. Some of the cars were still whole, just turned upside down. Others had their doors ripped off, or roofs torn apart. The climb was going to be more than a tough hike, nearly mountaineering. Jagged bits stuck out of it in all sorts of directions making it all the more dangerous. Like scaling a cactus wall. The last thing in the world he wanted was an infection from a cut. To compensate, Toy dressed in all of the extra clothes he brought on the trip. It restricted his movements and made him hot but he had no choice.

Getting onto the first car at the base of the pile turned out to be the hardest part since he needed to pull his full weight up by grabbing onto the wheel of an upturned van half submerged in the water. Once onto the van he climbed in stages one car at a time, searching for handholds. They were plentiful and he climbed with practiced speed like he had covered the same route before. The side mirrors of cars were particularly good handholds and once he climbed to an Audi above the van there were a series of footholds that gave his shoulder muscles a break. After an easier couple of steps up to a Mercedes perched at the very top, he grabbed onto the door handle to get steadied.

The door swung open.

Toy found himself hanging twenty feet above the water, too shocked to register what was going on at first. He didn't have time to be frightened. The last thing he wanted was to drop into the water, but that was exactly what was going to happen if it didn't get back onto the jetty. He might be cut to pieces by whatever lurked under the surface.

"No swimming. I won't".

Even if he was sure it was safe dropping into the water wasn't an option. He'd never jumped off the diving board during the free moments of the famous short-lived swim lessons. Instead, he crawled out of the pool and into the sun under a towel to dry off. The best part about the outdoor pool down the street from his house was lying on the concrete beside the concession stand in the warm yellow sun. He wished for that weaker sun again.

He had to make a decision fast. He reached up with one leg to wrap it around the open door window but missed. He tried a second time and just managed to snag his ankle onto the car door window frame. Using it for leverage he pulled himself up. Though he didn't weigh much, the stress on the door caused it to buckle. It felt as though the door would snap off at any second, and he didn't want it falling on top of him if he hit the water. In a desperate move he half-scrambled and half leaped toward the passenger seat and got almost all the way there. One second he was in the air, nearly flying and the next he was flailing. It was the seatbelt that saved him.

He missed the seat but got caught up to his elbow with the shoulder strap. Still hanging, but from the belt this time, he was a little closer to the car seat. He had to use all of his remaining strength to pull his dangling body high enough to reach a leg into the front seat. Finally, he collapsed onto the black leather bench of a red 1973 Chevelle. He slid over to the driver's side to catch his breath and to get further from the water.

The last time he sat in the driver's seat was at the Wimpy Burger drive-in, when Momndad would let him pretend he could drive. He knew little about driving except that you looked in the rearview mirror a lot, and Toy could never understand how it was possible to look back while driving forward. He loved sitting in the driver's seat at Wimpy's when the burgers and fries came. The attendant gave him a wink while hooking the orange plastic tray to the rolled down window, while Momndad sat together in the back. He closed his eyes. He was all by himself in the front seat, thinking about a future when he could pull up to a drive-in just like that one. Waiting for the food to arrive as the warm summer breeze silently brushed his hair was almost worth the eventual price.

When he opened them again he looked out the window. Instead of the metal box where you ordered your food, he saw a crush of sharp and twisted car parts whose handholds actually made it possible for an ascent to the top of the heap. Toy was stunned when he finally got to the top of the metal jetty. He was expecting to see land far off into the distance but instead it was only the shifting dunes of the sea. Huge swells overtaking one another in a bid to break themselves against the jetty, the Ferris wheel's long-range defense system.

In disbelief, Toy watched as the ocean surged in massive swells on the other side of the jetty. They smashed against the manmade reef, trying to climb to the top. Each one after the other getting a little higher as if climbing on the back of the previous wave. But on the fifth wave the four that came before it simply gave up and the whole water structure fell apart in a huge foamy pit. Then after a momentary rest, the pattern started all over again with the first of five waves. Never getting quite to the top of the far side of the jetty. It was clear that nothing of nature was going to overturn the accidental metal creation. No show of force would pull apart the twisted wreckage of the automobiles. In his hand was the bottle with the message he had been waiting to toss so he reached back tossed it as far as it would go into the huge waves. It was a statement, a statement he lost sight of almost immediately.

The jetty was a fortress that prevented anything from passing. And as Toy laughed at the irony – being protected on the Ferris wheel by the very thing that had helped bring forth an era lost to time – he saw on the horizon a range of black clouds. A storm raging.

"I'm not waiting around to see if that mess is coming this way."

Toy worried that Cyril was no match for a storm this intense. Even if it brought waves half the size of those on the other side of the jetty he was doomed. Waiting it out in one of the cars was not a good option, either. If Cyril was damaged or destroyed or swept away he'd be really trapped here. Plus, he had no food. Abandoning the jetty meant giving up all hope of finding land but there was no way he could sail on those massive waves. He believed that Momndad were out there in the direction the heron flew, past the un-crossable sea. Otherwise he had to admit where he got the family picture from. And he didn't want to go there. And still, going back to the Ferris wheel felt like giving up.

"I know there is a place for me, but I don't know how to get there."

It was beyond his reach. All he really wanted to know more than anything was if they were looking for him. And he had to face facts.

"Maybe, they're not."

He was out of time. He couldn't stay here in the protection of the Chevelle's front bench. He thought of only one thing, getting back to the Ferris wheel before the storm. It was the only safe place left. The storm had shifted the direction of the wind, pushing him back in the general direction of the Ferris wheel. But the storm was coming on very quickly, gaining on him with every minute.

He yelled down to Cyril, "The storm can push us back the way we came unless it gets too close. We're getting out of here, now."

He looked at his Timex to plot an hour's sail back in the direction he came when the alarm went off.

"Great timing. I'm way ahead of you." Toy figured that they would be in the general area of the Ferris wheel at about half past six. Well before dark if things went according to plan.

The storm was moving quickly. He jumped into Cyril and pulled open the sail. Immediately it filled with air and the swan leapt forward. They were navigating directly away from the jetty, with Toy roughly aiming in the direction of where he thought he would find the Ferris wheel. But since he could see only the horizon there was really no telling if he was going in exactly the right direction. If he miscalculated in only the smallest fraction then it would be multiplied more and more the further he went. He might even miss his target without even knowing it. The only thing he had going for him was that the Ferris wheel wasn't a moving target. Moving targets were much harder to hit.

"What do you mean, impossible? It was way harder for the astronauts since they were moving and so was the moon." Toy knew that the astronauts needed to hit a moving target, the moon, with another moving object, the ship. So they aimed ahead of where they were supposed to land.

"I know they had a computer. Well, we have... we have math. Sort of." It should be much easier for Toy since he was a single bullet shot at a single and immobile target. If the math worked out correctly then everything would be fine.

"Okay, I know my math class didn't cover those time and distance questions yet. I know I said that it was dumb and that nobody ever needed to know how long it would take a boat to sail between two islands seven hundred miles apart. We'll just have to guess."

Cyril looked at Toy suspiciously.

"Yes, a guess in math. There can be guesses in math y'know."

Every once in a while he turned back to check on the storm. The black clouds were gathering, attracted to each other. Still off in the distance but preparing something big. Toy felt incredibly exposed on the water, chased by a ferocious storm and sailing in an uncovered swan. The wind was pushing him along much faster than the trip to the jetty so his guess was definitely going to be off.

"Okay, not the best guess. But hopefully close enough." But deep in his heart Toy knew that hope wasn't much of a plan. So he checked his watch again. Just after six. As he did this he was distracted by a strange smell. It smelled like a campfire. But he couldn't really be sure because he had never been to camp.

Actually it smelled more like the time Mr. Burges the next door neighbor started a bonfire of leaves in his backyard. Momndad could see this was a bad idea and knew how it would end. At least that's what they said later. Together they called the police to complain. Before anything could happen to change things, the flames leapt onto Mr. Burges's deck. It was brand new, and had a fresh coat of finish on it. The tacky-to-the-touch one coat walnut brown deck stain exploded in shades of orange and blue. The flames burst three feet into the air. Toy stood on his own deck only thirty feet away, hopping up and down in excitement. Nothing that thrilling ever happened in the backyard. He could not take his eyes off the burning deck, the fire spread so quickly. The smell was the thing he remembered most vividly. He was probably five years old when that happened and he had not thought of it since.

The smell brought back the scene of Mr. Burges running with his garden hose and the firemen pushing him aside to get at it with theirs. The power of the water coming from the firehoses was staggering. Toy was dragged inside the house by his wrist to keep him out of the way. He was angry at not being able to watch the devastation. He wanted to see who was going to win, the firemen or the fire. The spray of all that water didn't put the fire out right away, so it looked to Toy like there was fire in the water itself. It just kept burning. The next day after everything calmed down, the deck and the back room of Mr. Burges's house was charred black and soaking wet. Toy remembered wondering how something could be wet and on fire at the same time.

At half past six, Toy started to get worried because the Ferris wheel was nowhere in sight. He tried to stay calm.

"We're not lost. Let's give it another five minutes." Maybe it was wishful thinking but he thought if he concentrated very hard, he could make the Ferris wheel simply appear on the horizon. But nothing.

The tiny hairs on the back of his neck stood up with a tingling sensation. It felt like he left his body and could hear himself talking. The biggest problem was that he didn't know which way to turn Cyril. Left or right. One of them was wrong and he could wind up even farther away from the safety of the Ferris wheel. And the storm was still getting closer every minute.

He checked on the storm again, and it was definitely getting closer. Moving in a direct line from the jetty.

"So you think we're off course and need to adjust to the right a little? You're sure?"

Toy changed course as agreed. He trusted Cyril even though he didn't have much faith in a swan's grasp of geometry. Rain started to pelt down one drop at a time and Toy noticed the drops were mixed with black ash.

A Cave on the Moon

Toy thought he was sailing on the surface of the moon as he scanned the flat horizon. The moon missions that fascinated Mom*n*dad when they were young regularly came up in dinner conversations. They were avid star gazers. Mom*n*dad met in science class where they discovered a dual love of astronomy. After that first meeting, they decided to enroll in more science courses together. From that point on they did everything together, like twins. They liked astrophysics the best. Their favorite thing to say was that they were inseparable, like twin moons endlessly revolving around each other in a timeless planetary orbit. Toy knew they graduated with astrophysics degrees and that they both got jobs at the same company. A company not in their field.

"Space was out of style", they said, and so getting hired on at Mutual Assurance, the insurance company, to 'crunch numbers' wasn't so bad. Crunching numbers, or as Toy liked to say 'crushing numbers', was easy for them. They loved solving math problems. Working at the insurance company paid the bills and gave them the time to be passionate about space and each other.

Toy listened to them talk endlessly about the solutions that NASA came up with to get the first three astronauts to the moon. They said it was all about the trajectory. Instead of aiming the mission capsule at the moon, they needed to aim it to where the moon was going to be at a certain place sometime in the future. In order to do that you had to track the moon's speed and trust that the empty space you were headed towards would be occupied by the target when you got there.

Toy thought about the astronauts as he held Cyril's sail on the ocean's flat surface. He felt like he was in his own mission capsule trying to aim at the general vicinity of the Ferris wheel. But he had no idea if he was doing it right. It was all guess work and no math. A solo traveler out of Houston's reach, and unable to communicate.

Not long after changing course, something appeared in the

distance. At first he thought it was the Ferris wheel but as he got closer he saw that he was wrong.                    "Anything is better than nothing."

He steered Cyril directly at the large shape, with the storm bearing down on him. The rain coupled with the black ash was already upon them. The ash made the visibility limited so Toy could barely see the pyramidal shape on the horizon until it he was nearly crashing into it. The rocky outcropping jutted out of the water dramatically. It was hardly an island at all since it was completely made of grey rock. Empty of trees but with smatterings of small bushy plants.

"Maybe they have berries."

Naturally, he worried that they'd be poisonous. He had no way of knowing one way or the other and guessed he'd have to eat one to see if it made him sick. As he pulled up very close the clouds opened up fully in an extreme downpour. As though a firehose had been turned on suddenly. The rain was the dark grey shade of ash. He was soaked completely through.

Up close, Toy saw that the sides of the rock formation were steep with many facets sticking out in odd directions. As if its maker was trying to fake a convincing mountaintop. Blocky and unnatural. Toy took down the sail and paddled around looking for some kind of shelter. As he came around the far side he noticed a short piece of railway track shooting out of a large opening. The track protruded from an opening on the side of the structure. A tunnel. The hole was like a mine entrance and was big enough for Toy to climb inside. But not for Cyril.

"You'll have to wait outside. I'll tie you up to the track so you'll be safe. I won't let anything bad happen to you."

Toy kept Cyril on a very short line so he wouldn't bang into the track too hard if the storm was as violent as it looked. The wind gusted suddenly and he narrowly escaped slipping back into the water where he would have been carried off with the current.

Once inside the cave entrance the sounds outside grew muffled and Toy felt oddly detached from the storm like he was listening to it on the radio. Mostly, he was grateful to be out of the wind and rain, though he had to contend with clothes so wet they felt like dishtowels after doing the dinner plates. He still had on all of the layers he brought with him, so he removed the outer ones and lay them out to dry in the cave. Then, he sat at the edge of the entranceway and marveled at how the rain pushed sideways in the intense wind. The cave that Toy was inside didn't extend very far back but there was a ledge on one side of the tracks where he could sit. It took time for his eyes to adjust to the blackness. After that, he could see that the track angled steeply down into water toward the back of the cave. The back end was flooded and so front portion of the cave was habitable. The walls were rough, as if made from the same stuff as his old house. Scratchy like sandpaper. And bits of it were flaking off in places, so unlike real rocks at all. As he lay down on the ledge beside the track he waited patiently but couldn't fall sleep. It wasn't surprising. He was worried about Cyril out in the storm. The rain was coming down hard and would be filling it up with water. So Toy turned his back to the sandpaper wall, laying on his side, that he might keep an eye on the swan. He told himself it was to make sure Cyril didn't break free from the rope tied to the track. Being left stranded on the phony outcropping was a constant worry in the storm. But he kept telling himself it was really out of concern for Cyril's well-being.

"There's nobody around. I don't have to pretend that he isn't real."

He wasn't eleven anymore, the age when he stopped self-narrating playtime with his toys. After that he learned to keep secret the little voice inside of his head while Mom*n*dad were watching him play. Until now.

It rained so hard that a waterfall poured over the entrance-way, creating the impression that Toy was in that most secret of caves. It was damp, cold and uncomfortable.

"How did Neanderthals ever manage it?"

While the storm raged on into the evening, Cyril bobbed up and down smacking against the track. Each time Toy winced.

He was looking so intently at the swan that he hardly noticed at first that the rain continued but the sky cleared. Toy didn't think that was possible. To the music of the rain Toy watched the moon rise into an empty sky, an odd round frame around Cyril like a spotlight.

Thinking about moons and planets from the mouth of the cave Toy watched the huge white ball rise by tiny increments in the night sky. The storm wouldn't give up. The water around Cyril churned with abnormally high winds. The cave offered enough protection even though it was designed to offer none at all. It took Toy several hours to figure it out, but this was no mountaintop. He was hiding out in the mouth of the roller-coaster, the one he never rode. He failed to recognize it at first because the lower part of the ride, dressed up as a mountain, was completely underwater. And since he'd never ridden it, he had not seen up close the top part of the mouth where the cars full of screaming riders came shooting out into the daylight. The half-submerged track should have been the tipoff but it was instead the flaky walls that gave it away. Fake rocks covered in greyish brown stucco, a little spongy to the touch. He wouldn't have noticed any of this if the moon hadn't shone in like a searchlight illuminating the small interior.

Its light revealed all. Attached to the walls were all manner of mining tools, pickaxes, shovels, and chains. Toy excitedly pulled on a shovel intending to get it down. It wouldn't budge. Disappointed, he found it was as false as the walls themselves. All of it was an illusion and totally useless. So too, the plants must be equally fake and so there went the idea of getting edible berries from the bushes, even ones that might make him sick. So much fantasy made Toy wonder. Would anyone on the ride really see such detailed decoration in the tunnel while they were moving so fast?

He was lying on the hard ledge, looking out when a flash of lightning lit up the sky so fast Toy couldn't shut his eyes in time. The explosion turned everything white. A second later thunder exploded. Toy worried that it would hurt Cyril's ears or worse hit him directly. The swan was out in the storm with no protection at all. Toy was about to look away when the next bolt of lightning struck, and for a moment a brilliant and jagged vein connected the surface of the water to the heavens. The singular moment etched itself into Toy's eyes. Not his mind. Just his eyelids, so that when he closed them and put his hands over his ears the vein of lightning was burned in. Intense white light. That is how he found the Ferris wheel. In that image etched onto his eyelids he saw the tiny wheel struck by lightning. For the longest time he couldn't un-see it.

Toy had seen lightning storms before when he was very little. He watched from the living room, perched on the back of the couch by the window. He always had to wait patiently, because the long turns between lightning took a long time. He'd be playing on the floor with some plastic army men, and then out of the corner of his eye he'd see a white flash. Back then, he was rarely able to witness the lightning directly. He always seemed to be looking away at the wrong time. It was that way with lightning. It was a surprise every time. A jealously guarded secret. As massive as it was fast. Only a few times had he actually been rewarded with a true lightning show. And then all but one of those times it was the boring sheet lightning that just painted the black sky white. The one precious time he witnessed a truly forked tongue of lightning, just in the split second before it was gone, he was astonished. It was late and he was supposed to go to bed, but he pleaded with Momndad for another hour. They gave in to half and so he was getting super anxious that the storm would move on without a decent bolt. When it happened, Toy was still taken by surprised and wished he'd given up earlier. He ran up to bed without being asked. He lay under the blankets unable to fall asleep.

The lightning storm he was in was completely different than the one he remembered. A rabid change. Blast upon quicker blast, a bombardment of flashes that would not let the night return to its natural state. Toy felt his eyes burning out of their sockets. The intensity forced him to block his eyes with the palms of his hands as if the light was penetrating even into the false rock of the cave. Like a fireworks show coming to a climax the lightning stopped with a final echo. The one thing to remain was the lightning blast tattoo of the Ferris wheel on the inside of his eyelids.

The rain ceased but the wind made the water choppy and Toy wanted to get out of there at first light. But, he was afraid to chance a sailing. Cyril was riding low in the water and Toy needed time to bail some out. He had absolutely no choice but to wait.

Exhausted from the ordeal of the storm, Toy lay on the ledge. His eyes unable to close, he pictured himself in a small white dinghy sailing across an ocean of cerulean blue dunes each taller than the next. Hundreds of feet high, up one side and down the other. He noticed that the ocean was static like a desert but that was not the oddest thing. He was not in control of the dinghy as it rocketed up and down the massive blue mountains. It followed a set path, hidden to Toy but deliberate. He was passively going along for the ride. It was a lot like being in the back seat of Momndad's car on a Sunday drive in the country hills, unable to make a difference in the destination. He was used to their rambling for hours without end, unaware that the back seat was getting hotter and hotter in the noonday sun.

The sun roasted outside the cave. It heated up so fast that all of the wet clothes were completely dry. It was so hot that Toy, welcoming the slightest breeze, found it difficult to breathe like being in an dry sauna. His lungs felt heavy and on fire at the same time. When the feeling passed and the storm had completely moved on Toy climbed down to Cyril and began bailing him out with his left shoe. It wasn't a perfect tool but it was the only one he had because the captain's hat wasn't an option. It was more of a sieve and he needed it to protect himself from sunstroke.

The dream was still fresh in his mind so he decided to re-tell it to Cyril. It started off with the part about racing up and down the blue hills in the white dinghy. Toy sensed that Cyril was agitated about the dinghy being in the story. And then the retelling started to make very little sense because it was becoming impossible to relate the sense of urgency Toy felt in the dream. And so the story took a detour.

"After sailing the blue hills for the longest time I came upon a long stretch of marsh, full of tall green weeds and bulrushes. I sailed past some ducks floating in the wetlands and almost immediately bumped into a low shoreline. Curious, I leapt out of the boat and onto a green slope that lead up to a wide field of grass and sand. Kneeling down I took a handful of the sand and cast it to the wind. I started to walk. And walk some more. Then I came upon a village of little houses, like play structures in the schoolyard. They were colourful as if made of gingerbread, and decorated with all manner of candy canes, chocolate rings, jujubes, and gum drops. Some of them the size of watermelons. Walking through the village was strange because no one came out of any of the little gingerbread houses to greet me. I was about to knock on the door of the nearest tiny house when I noticed that it was not made of gingerbread at all. The house was made of Styrofoam and hard colorful plastic fading in the sun. The candy looked real enough to eat, and some of the chocolate rings were even melting in the sun. Just to be sure I licked one and it smelled miraculously like chocolate. But when I tried to take a bite it was hard, like plastic. It tasted real but wasn't edible.

Beyond the crop of tiny houses, there was an open field where I saw a huge black cloud. At first it looked like a storm on the horizon. But on closer inspection it was not a storm at all. The clouds were billowing the black smoke of a wildfire. A wildfire kicking up a tremendous wall of flame and smoke that blocked out the sun, fed by its heat. It seemed to turn, driving directly at me. It was like standing in an open field with lightning striking overhead, with no chance of escape.

Fire burst from the ground in gas explosions rolling into the sky. A wave of heat an apartment block high. It grew like a beanstalk, reaching into a black cloud, replenishing itself from below."

Toy got so carried away with the fantastic landscape in his mind that he began to get mixed up. He smelled the chocolate and candy of the plastic house. Awake and asleep were getting confused. How long had it been since he really slept? Popcorn and sleep were the two things driving him on toward the return trip to the Ferris wheel.

He checked that the sea was calm enough to set sail. Once Cyril was rigged up to go he quickly checked the swan's condition. It looked on the surface like it weathered the storm pretty well. Even though the storm had been incredibly intense with hurricane force winds, Cyril was at least in one piece. There were chips in the white paint on most of the body, the wings and tail but the head was unblemished. The paint on his left eye was chipped off and so it looked like he was in a perpetual wink. As if he had a secret that had to be kept even from Toy.

"I told you it would be okay. What a baby." Toy said smiling.

Climbing aboard and pushing off at the same time, he was surprised by how easy sailing had become. They barely bobbled as Toy sat down and pulled on the rope to open the sail. But, to his dismay Cyril limped along slowly rather than picking up his characteristic speed. Something was definitely wrong and it wasn't with Cyril.

After a few minutes he realized the wind was too weak for good sailing. Tacking into the wind took some time to figure out, but essentially he had to work his way back in a zig zag pattern and be really patient with the limited wind. Moving forward depended on going at it from an angle. It required precision. He got the hang of it but despite all of his patience and skill he had to admit that he wasn't getting very far.

"At this rate it will take forever. And no, I'm not blaming you. Did I say it was your fault? Yes, it's the wind. I know you're not in charge of the wind."

Toy didn't want to tell Cyril but the wind would have to pick up soon. He was getting hungrier. In short order the breeze died almost completely and Cyril came to rest, bobbing gently side to side. The sideways rocking movement of the swan made its fiberglass head sway even more profoundly. Toy started to feel a little sick. The motion gave the impression that Cyril was busy thinking deeply about something. The swan seemed to be mulling over that secret idea. The wink. Toy hoped that the secret had something to do with the wind coming back soon.

Far in the distance he could see the Ferris wheel, little more than a dot on the horizon. His North Star in daytime. He thought about paddling but it was too far, and he'd only succeed in getting exhausted. He was afraid to exert himself too much and become unable to sail when he needed his strength. He was feeling weaker so he sat patiently waiting.

And with so much time he began to think about April the ninth at twenty-two minutes after five. What was supposed to happen on that day? Or more correctly, what was to have already happened since that day had already passed. It wasn't a birthday, or anniversary or school holiday. The alarm went off once a day reminding him of his failure to figure the mystery out.

"Either everyone had incorrectly set their own watch alarm to a date long passed or maybe you did it," Cyril looked dubious. Then it dawned on him, "or I did it."

"Why would I set all the watch alarms, and why to the exact same time and date?" Cyril had the look that said Toy should already know the answer.

"Because I needed to get my attention. It's a warning about something that happened months ago, or is going to happen soon."

## Adventure Rides

Cyril drifted in the barely flowing current, more or less in the direction of the Ferris wheel. Toy sat passively in the seat feeling like he did on the kiddie rides that you only pretended to control. Nervous because they weren't getting to their destination, Toy started telling Cyril a different story.

"Did you know that there are only three kinds of rides in the park? Kiddie rides, thrill rides, and adventure rides. On a kiddie ride, like the spaceship, you just sit there as the vehicle did its thing. There are flashing knobs that create the illusion of having control but really they do nothing at all. Only the youngest kids are fooled by these. In fact, the spaceship is dragged along a track, making turns or going up a low rise to simulate the feeling of lift-off. The buzzes and beeps and flashes of light cover the truth. A passenger had no control whatsoever.

Thrill rides are essentially an upgraded version of the kiddie ride, but attaining super high speeds and even g-forces similar to those experienced by astronauts. I have absolutely no interest in thrill rides. I didn't care for the idea of being shot along a track at a million miles an hour at the mercy of gravity and engineers who've moved onto another project by the time this one was assembled. And I'm way beyond kiddie rides. They are an embarrassment that I figured out last summer."

Painfully that awakening happened on a kiddie ride itself. One moment Toy was happy to climb into the spaceship and its alluring mission control. After a few revolutions he sickened at the fake knobs and Toy became self-conscious that adults were looking at him funny. He was sure they were thinking he was too old for the spaceship. The look on his face said it all. Like you, I know this spaceship is fake, except I'm the one riding on it. But I assure you, it's for the last time.

Toy continued, "adventure rides are a different thing, in a class by themselves. An adventure ride is something you drive by yourself. Bumper cars are adventure rides because they let you drive in any direction, but at achingly slow speeds. Some drivers go in reverse by turning the wheel as far as it will go in one direction. Reverse always goes a little bit faster. Best of all it takes the other drivers by surprise. The reverse rear-ender is the best move of all. The trouble is that there are always an immense number of cars jammed into the bumper cars area so you can hardly move at all. There's no freedom in that. Too many cars. More cars, more money.

The swan ride, on the other hand, is pure freedom. You line up on a real wooden dock while the attendant hooked the next swan in line on his long pole. Gingerly you climb into the flat-bottomed swan while the attendant explains how the motorized control works. A small lever between the seats can be turned left or right to guide the swan on the freest of paths. The swan's domain is a huge pond of real water, which means real danger. If you stand up in the swan, the attendant warns, you will definitely fall into the water."

No more threatening buildup was necessary to impart to Toy that the swan was the most terrifying ride in the park. But also the only ride that allowed complete freedom to roam. Despite his fear of the water, which he had to put in the back of his mind, he trusted the swan to provide a new experience each time. He rode it thirty-two times the summer before the Ferris wheel.

"Then there is the Ferris wheel, itself. It alone stands apart from all other rides. It can't be classified. Its motion is predictable but it behaves randomly. It stops frequently and strands unlucky riders at the very top for who knows how long while unsuspecting passengers get on at the bottom. There is always the fear of being stuck at the top if the motor malfunctions," his voice trailed off.

"Plus there are no seatbelts on the Ferris wheel. I bet people who ride it for the first time are freaked out by that," he stated more pragmatically.

Like the swan, falling out was always a possibility. But there was a significant difference between the two types of ride. The swan had autonomy so you could go almost anywhere, but the Ferris wheel was a thing unto itself. Toy obsessed about it over the summer when he distanced himself from the spaceship rides once and for all. He had spent the entire year building up the courage.

As Cyril and Toy inched forward as the iconic silhouette of the Ferris wheel came into sharper focus. The view from the side. It was still only the size of his hand and appeared to float on the horizon but Toy knew how suddenly the perspective could shift once he got a little closer. His wish for a breeze went unanswered. Untying the paddle from Cyril's tail, he finally leaned over the side to get things moving. There was no choice but to give up on the wind. He'd have to do it himself. As he shifted to the side of the flat seat, he noticed an inch of water at his feet that wasn't there before.

"There was probably a little left behind when I bailed you out."

"No cause for alarm," Toy lied. "It's because I'm leaning to one side to paddle. It makes the little bit of water seem like more. But it's not."

Choppy waves splashed up on Cyril's side but the wind wasn't picking up. Paddling against the churning water was even harder and after only a few minutes Toy was exhausted. His shoulders burned. But the Ferris wheel was getting closer now, maybe twice the size of his fist. Catching his breath he bent over his feet and that was when he saw the water inside the swan was almost at his ankle.

"Problem," was all he could think of saying.

A problem he wished was happening in slow motion, but it wasn't. It was unfolding much faster.

"Why did we wait for wind for so long? If I had started paddling right away we'd be there by now."

The back of his neck tensed up. He was holding his breath without realizing it. He had made a terrible miscalculation. He thought he had more time. In the back of his mind he knew Cyril was taking on water but he had denied it. The water was above his ankles. Bailing was useless.

The wind abandoned him. It felt like the forces of nature were conspiring against him, preventing him from returning to the Ferris wheel. He had to paddle. And faster.

Paddling wildly. He thought back to his hasty inspection of Cyril after the storm. He should have been more careful. He should have looked more closely for cracks since Cyril had bounced around in the storm pretty hard all night. There was now visible a crack on the inside middle of Cyril's white body. Thin, almost imperceptible, but long like a hair. He should have seen it. It bubbled like the bath. Toy's shoulders still ached. There was nothing in the craft to throw out like in the movies when a boat was sinking. He couldn't lighten the load unless he threw himself out.

The Ferris wheel was getting closer but still at least a football field away. Too far to swim. He was going slower now that Cyril had taken on so much water. The added weight tore at the muscles on his back. His mouth was dry but he didn't have time to rest. If he stopped it might be impossible to get started again.

"Come on. We're going to make it."

The slower his progress the faster the water rose. It was nearly half filled. With so much water on board Toy was surprised that Cyril hadn't sunk. He pushed ahead not knowing what else to do. Thinking that he could make it to the final destination just at the last second, as though running to the bathroom. He always made it just in time. He thought the exact same thing until he was about a pool's length from the metal beam of the Ferris wheel.

Having taken on so much water, Cyril's crack opened inches wide. Before Toy had time to register the implications the swan split completely in half and they were both fully immersed. The tail end of the swan slipped silently and quickly below the surface. Cyril's front bobbed lifelessly on the surface and Toy grabbed for his neck. He refused to cry out something like 'No. Don't' go. Don't leave me by myself.' Those were the exact words running through his mind but he refused to say them out loud.

He held on with both hands, as the swan looked into Toy's eyes.

"Sorry," was all Toy quietly squeaked out. Barely above a whisper. And then Cyril dropped below the surface.

Toy wanted to redo it over again, but there was no going back. He had badly misjudged it all. He underestimated the distance, he went off without a plan, he pushed ahead when he knew he should wait, and he didn't check that Cyril was safe. And so he was caught completely unprepared. He didn't have a backup plan because he was so certain he'd make it. He thought all of this in the space of a second.

"I thought there was more time." The clock had already run out.

The water was up to Toy's neck in an instant. He opened his mouth to scream at his loss but he swallowed the same black water that dragged Cyril to the sandy bottom. There was no telling how deep it was, unlike the pool which had printed reminders on the side every few feet. Numerical warnings of going too far. All he knew was that his feet couldn't touch the bottom and, like the swan, he wasn't floating anymore.

To Toy, it was the swim lessons all over again except there was no poolside to grab. He was stranded in the middle of nowhere and he was being forced to confront past failures. It was true that he often held the floating rope or stood on the bottom when he was supposed to be treading water. He hardly thought it was cheating but the swim teacher said Toy was only hurting himself. Toy denied to himself that there would one time come a day when he'd need swim skills. Holding onto something was not setting up a future disaster, he had once thought. Alone in the ocean there was nothing to cheat with anymore. The past caught up with him at the absolute worst moment. He tried to dog-paddle since that was the only stroke he learned, aiming directly for the base of the Ferris wheel. Short arm and leg movements were all he could muster. His clothes were wet. He should be able to float but wet clothes tried to drag him under and it made him even more tense. Panicked. He was plagued with the two things that prevented forward movement. He never mastered a single one of the swim strokes where the best he could do was flail around in the water trying to keep his face dry. The single embarrassing achievement was not nearly enough to see Toy awarded one of the neatly stitched badges. The other kids all accelerated to the next grade.

Toy's dog-paddle stroke was all that was keeping his head above the water, pulling him slowly toward metal beam X-33. There were no badges on this test, only survival. His two little arms were tiring rapidly. Finally, he was no more than twenty feet away but it felt like a mile. His shoulders gave out and he could not move forward even an inch.

Slowing meant sinking. The water got up to his mouth and then he slipped under. It was not like he imagined drowning would be. It wasn't the arms flailing around in the air that was seen on TV. All of the action happened below the surface. Just below the water's surface was where the panic waited.

A few weeks after he turned six, he was at a beach by a river he took for an ocean. The river seemed massive but it wasn't wider than a football field. The bank of trees and beach on the other side was easily visible. Bigger kids could swim to the other side. Toy had to stay on the babyish beach with the picnic blankets, and hot dog stands, and the lifeguard in his impossibly tall red metal tower equipped with umbrella. The bigger kids got to explore the wilderness on the far side.

The river was out in the country a long drive away. Toy rode there in the back of Gramma and Papa's station wagon with the watermelons they bought at a roadside stand. While the car was unpacked, Toy noticed children were digging with plastic pails and shovels making muddy sandcastles. Architecture that barely held its form, melting in the sun. He had no shovel or pail. No one thought to bring one for him. Gramma and Papa liked to sit in the shade, and left Toy to do as he pleased.

Finding himself far away from the safety of the picnic blanket he fell among kids he never met before. He didn't introduce himself to the strange kids. Instead, he just stood there quietly, watching and trying to understand what it was they were doing. His stillness attracted attention all the same. He only wanted to watch them, but they weren't having it. They began posturing and posing, shooting insults at one another just for laughs and seeing Toy's awkwardness they circled around him. None of them wanted him spying. They pushed him. Called him weird. Before he knew what was happening he was face down on the beach with his mouth in a puddle. Coughing. Someone he couldn't see was holding him down but he could see that the others turned away to leave. Whether they were frightened away or just got bored he was finally able to rise up out of the puddle. He had something in his hands the weight of a watermelon. He lifted it above his head. He would show them how strong he was and then they would leave him alone. Their shocked faces. He felt weightless as it left his hands. The watermelon hit the ground with a thud of finality. It didn't crack open. It embedded itself an inch or two into the sand, and yet its juice was leaking out onto the sand. It made a small but rapidly growing red puddle. All of the children had run away except one who stood stiffly over the watermelon, his arms by his side, his fingers spread, and his mouth open. Nothing came out. His foot was pinned under it. As they ran away, a few children screamed and Toy could hear them. He looked down at the boy's foot to see there was no watermelon. It was a large wide flat rock. The group of kids ran, disappearing around a grassy sand dune. Left behind, Toy stared at the foot caught under the rock. There was red everywhere. Toy turned and walked away. The kids were all gone. He walked back to the picnic blanket, numb.

When he got back to the blanket everyone was gone. Not just Grandma and Papa. Everyone. All their food was left out in the sun. Half-eaten sandwiches and an uncovered plastic potato salad container. Invading ants were crawling over the black and red plaid blanket and into the plastic containers. Other people's abandoned blankets had similar armies of ants crawling freely over their food. Yet, the beach wasn't completely deserted. Only the very small kids were left sitting in the hot sun, playing obliviously in the sand with blue and red plastic shovels and pails.

Toy looked toward the other side of the river and saw a long line of adults that had all joined hands in a huge people chain. It extended from Toy's side of the beach to the wilderness side. It looked like they were going to have a race. But there was no finish line. Then, they started to walk, slowly and still holding hands, with those in the middle of the river up to their chests. The river water was muddy brown because there was little current. Walking blindly in the murky water, the adults had to feel around with their feet for the child that was lost.

Toy heard the lifeguard speak through a bullhorn from her chair perched on the metal tower. People didn't really need instructions because it happened every weekend. Everyone knew the drill. When a kid went missing for a while the lifeguard blew the whistle and the adults fell into formation. But it was a drill with no result. No one ever turned up in the water. Lost kids usually came out of a hiding place in a bush or from behind the food stand. After a sharp word or a smack from angry parents life went back to normal.

The line finished up at the floated rope boundary having found nothing, which was a momentary relief, and the lifeguard blew her whistle. All clear. Everyone came out of the water. The kids went back to their blankets on the beach, brushed away the ants, and returned to the routine of snacking. It was a ritual that seemed to take up much of an afternoon.

Everyone participated in the chain. No one ever dreamed of taking that opportunity to leave the area, to pack up their car and just go home. Nobody had the nerve to abandon another family, even strangers. Even the kids knew that.

The one time it took much longer for the second all clear whistle to blow, the one that told the kids to back in the water, there was only silence. The river was still. Frozen.

"They aren't going to find anything", Toy said out loud to no one. "He's not in the water. Or playing in the woods."

The air was hushed. People looked in all sorts of directions expectantly. It was like a moment of silence before something traumatic happens and no one realizes it until later. Everything had been going so well at the river for such a very long time. Everything had been the same for so long that people were caught by surprise at exactly the same time. And if they were asked later on, years later, they all recalled the same memory whether it was that they saw it directly or heard about it later. The one thing everyone agreed on who retold the story was that there was no blood coming from the boy's feet. It was his long blonde hair covered in red that everyone was sure about. It pooled on the yellow sand.

The Towel

The water was freezing cold. Though the air had been un-bearably hot, the water was ice. Toy was still holding his breath underwater. Pressing his lips together was hard because he was getting cold. He thought about his warm blanket that he hid under at the pool while the other kids had their swim lessons. Toy felt safe under his towel, his protective cape with the picture of a cartoon space alien on it. Underneath the alien was printed 'take me to your leader'. He was small enough that the small towel covered his whole body except for his feet, his pristine feet.

The swim instructors joked about his dry feet sticking out from under the towel as they walked past him on the pool deck. He could hear them say you had to keep moving to avoid freez-ing to death in the ocean. Even though he didn't get in the water Momndad made him come to the classes. It was odd not getting in the pool for swim lessons called 'Get Wet'. But they paid for the lessons and weren't offered a refund so he had to attend them all. He learned the story about staying safe in the pool by heart from the safety of his 'take me to your leader' towel. He lay under the same towel, once before on the beach, trying not to be seen. He kept his mouth shut though he wanted to scream.

The same scream was trying to get out of his mouth, under-water, but instead he forced open his eyes. They burned from the salt water, like a bath of tears. So like the bath he had been hastily thrust into when Momndad discovered some splashes of blood on his arms and his swimsuit after the beach. Grandma and Papa were at a loss to explain where it all came from. Momndad ran the bath and left plodding downstairs to see Gramma and Papa out the door without a word. Toy and his boats were left alone in the warm bath while the tension in the front hall built to a peak. The silence felt like it was about to erupt so Toy held his breath want-ing not to be taken off his guard. He kept thinking that words like knives would burst from the hallway. But nothing. Silence. The bath was left to run. And run. The boats floated to the very top of the white porcelain lip and then over onto the floor in a waterfall. He sat there in the warm bath up to his neck raising no alarm. Holding his breath. He saw the boats float over the edge of the bath and onto the floor, moving silently out the door and heading for the stairs. Momndad discovered him sitting in the overflowing bath with the water up to his chin. He never found out about any of what really happened with the boy or the rock or the watermelons. Everyone seemed to want to forget.

The silence and the cold under the water made it easy to forget. He forgot the Ferris wheel. He forgot the park. But he couldn't forget Momndad. Where were they now? Why didn't they just appear like they did when he got lost in kiddieland. He could barely recall their voices, it was so quiet under the water. Like a soundproof room. It wasn't cold anymore. The same warmth had returned to his body floating inches below the surface of the ocean, mere feet away from the base of the Ferris wheel.

Toy heard the instructors at the pool yell, "Kick hard". He had always given up too soon, never getting to try. He was angry that the other kids were able to stay in the pool and follow instructions. He wanted them, anyone, to plead with him to come and give it another chance. But no one did. The instructors respected his wishes to stay out of the pool, even though that wasn't what he really wanted. He wanted them to challenge him to jump back in and he wanted to be the hero. But instead they just ignored him. Invisible under the towel.

The noises of everything around him rushed back all at once, the wind, the waves, and the screeching of the Ferris wheel's metal joints. The same screeching from one girl alone on the beach. In fright it was impossible to tell the difference between the rollercoaster and the beach. The downhill scream that fades as the rollercoaster shoots up the far corner. No one ever screamed on their way up the first big hill. Novice riders held their breath and let it out on the way down. Released in a shout. In the valley where the screams were left. And on multiple turns on the same ride, eventually riders screamed out of ritual not fear.

Boredom. Everyone got used to the fall.

In the water nobody was watching at all. Even the heron was gone. And Cyril. Poor Cyril. And nobody was there to see him admit to throwing the rock. He never found out what happened to the child. And nobody ever knew who did it. But here in the water, only feet away, he at least admitted it to himself. He did it. He didn't even know that kid. It was too late to take back. Toy screamed out. So, with no one watching he kicked his feet. Hard. His head was out of the water, so that he looked like a duck moving on the surface of a pond. His arms were spreading the water and the carpet aside as his legs propelled him forward. He didn't stop until he hit his head on X-33.

Holding onto the submerged cage of the gondola car where he once fished, ankle deep in water, he was relieved.

"Finally."

He couldn't remember how he climbed back up to his old perch. He sat there intent on the horizon, never blinking for who knew how long. The first thought that came to his conscious mind was; change.

## Change

Toy noticed that many of the plastic bottles were beginning to stick together, formed into globs in the melting sun. The largest of the globs contained empty and full water bottles alike and had also swallowed up pieces of wood and a dead seagull. He picked up a group of bottles infected with the black glueyness. It wouldn't wash off his hands.

"I'm sunk if this happens to all of the drinking water."

Using the long pole he pushed the huge plastic blobs away. Right away he found that he could see deeper into the water than ever before. He expected to find fish. None.

"Is a large body of water empty of fish an ocean at all?"

Meandering under the surface was instead a thicker black ribbon. Something was feeding it to make it grow. The cause was still a mystery but it was clearly messing up his food. He needed to do something, but what? Not only did he have no solution but he wasn't sure of the problem. But, he did know that he didn't want to face it. So, he spent the rest of the afternoon in the gondola organizing his remaining packages. Everything he had for food was stacked up according to type and size. There was enough to last for a few weeks, but then he would have to go fishing again. If the black ribbon ruined the carpet then he'd be in really big trouble. When he finished counting up the bags he moved on to the change. Counting it all up there was more than thirty dollars. What he was going to do with the money was unclear. Just having the change reminded him of Momndad because of the insurance company where they both worked. Mutual Assurance. Once, it ran a television commercial that showed a hand stacking pocket change with the slogan, "people rarely change, and Mutual Assurance is people". The idea behind the advertisement was that for pennies a day you could insure your home, your car and your life. Toy always wondered what the person attached to the hand in the ad looked like, assuming it was the owner of Mutual Assurance. Toy couldn't understand how you could insure your life from bad things any more than he could grasp that Mutual was one of the largest multinationals on the little blue planet with shareholdings in every major portfolio.

But he thought he understood the message in the slogan, that the company Momndad both worked for would always be there. Stable. Eternal. Timeless. The company would never change. That slogan used to give Toy some comfort knowing that Momndad could work there as long as they wanted. Other kids had parents without jobs so he felt lucky. Momndad's jobs had been a growing source of dinner conversation in the weeks leading up to the Ferris wheel. Either they talked about living off the company pension when they got older or they fretted over the latest policies and rules. Most of it went way over Toy's head but he learned all he needed to know from the tone of their voices. There were angry voices when the company announced the latest pay cut. There was grief when a hurricane levelled that distant island. They tried to hide it from Toy by talking in complex words he might not understand, and it was true that he didn't, but the sound of their voices gave it all away.

The thing they talked about the most was how Mutual Assurance made money. Toy heard Momndad say that Mutual made money by selling life insurance to young people. The odds were against those people dying young. And older folks usually cancelled their policies so Mutual was a money black hole. Cash went in, never escaping.

The hockey card scam at school operated the same. The boys at school of all ages collected hockey cards but the trouble was that there were many doubles of lesser players. No one could get a full team. Someone was always missing. The older boys hatched a plan to fix this problem. They convinced all of the kids including the little ones to put their doubles in one big pot. By paying into the hockey card pot you could take a card for free in order to complete your favorite team. But, in practice the younger kids rarely got to withdraw the cards they wanted since they weren't in charge. The older kids got whatever they wanted. One day, all of the little kids asked for their cards back from the pot at the exact same time. The card game collapsed the same week Mutual did.

That was the day Mom*n*dad's dinner conversation tone grew serious. If Toy knew the word to describe it he would have said 'dire'. They couldn't crush the numbers fast enough to keep up with the run on policies. Too many storms and accidents. A whole town full of people died. Mutual Assurance was straining under the weight of paying out on lost homes, restaurants, office buildings, and people. Normally, a single plane crash was not such a big deal, even though it triggered over a hundred policies. Plus the paper on the airplane itself. Mutual held policies on all of it. So, more frequent high cross winds were responsible for more crashes than ever before, though it didn't stop people from flying or dissuade the airlines from pursuing profits. Planes crashed more frequently but Mom*n*dad just crushed new numbers. More houses burned in summer wildfires than the summer before. Mom*n*dad found new numbers. Nobody thought it was a crisis. People denied it was a problem at all. Big companies had their ups and downs. It was normal. When it was too almost late Toy remembered asking if there was something that could fix it. And Mom*n*dad answered with a laugh, "a time machine."

The day before leaving for the amusement park, Toy helped paint a picket sign for the protest at Mutual's office tower. Twin signs. On the front was written "Mutual" and on the back "Assured Destruction". It was Toy's idea and he thought it was clever. But when they arrived at the offices downtown only a scattering of people showed up. He was disappointed that there weren't hordes of angry people chanting and marching. Instead, the small gathering of folks looked much more like a line of picketing strikers angry about their working conditions. The roads weren't closed to the usual traffic in front of the tower. Cars just drove past without paying an ounce of attention.

In the news it hadn't been made at all clear why Mutual was to blame for anything. It was a massive company owned by no one in particular but instead in small pieces by everyone. Whoever was a shareholder. And since it was bankrupt there were no feet to lay the blame at. The company just sold policies. To protect folks when disaster struck. Unless you looked into where the profits were invested. Car makers, oil companies, manufacturing plants. Not a single wind farm. It was completely two-faced. If a corporation had a face.

Thinking about the face and reverse of those picket signs, Toy's hands fiddled with the coins. Change was two-sided and dual faced, too. A head and a tail. Two opposing things happening at the same time, like fire in water. Fire and water mixed together. Toy learned that you could prevent water from dousing fire if there was an accelerant present. Momndad said people used it to deliberately burn their houses down for the insurance money. A normal fire was not that hard to put out, so if you wanted to make sure that the firefighters weren't able to douse the flames you added an accelerant, like gasoline. Professional arsonists used gasoline mixed with frozen orange juice to create a homemade version of napalm that could burn under water. But insurance investigators were able to find traces of the accelerant. Pros usually got away with it but not amateurs like Mr. Burges. A bonfire. Really. "Next time", said the fire marshal, "do us a favour and make it a flood."

Momndad figured it out easily. They were great amateur insurance detectives. But detectives are only good at piecing together the past, not predicting the future. Their science couldn't handle what was coming. And that is why they were totally taken by surprise when Mutual Assurance went bankrupt. The biggest surprise for them came too late. Worse of all, there was no plan to change anything that might put some balance back into the game. It was out of control. And so Mutual Assurance died. Overnight. Momndad lost their jobs both at the same time on the same Monday.

While he was lost in the past the watch alarm went off, again.

"Great. Twenty-two minutes after five, again. For whatever good that'll do."

He had given up thinking something was supposed to happen. The alarm off every day and nothing ever happened. He had been ignoring it for days. For a minute he thought he might be reliving the same day over and over again. Maybe when he blanked out he awoke to the same day, April the ninth.

"That's totally idiotic."

If not that, then what? Every day was the same on the Ferris wheel as the day before. There was no science that told him the days were progressing. The stars were in the same place each night. The sun and moon chased each other across the sky. And then the proof came to him out of nowhere. It was a different day if the sun rose at a slightly later time than the day before. He would start making note of it tomorrow. But with the rapidly growing globs of black ribbon he knew in his heart he was out of time.

He was so tired. He ached of thinking. Climbing back up to his perch the stenciled letters and numbers on the beams caught his eye. X-33. Letters and numbers. Puzzles. Codes. Patterns. The puzzle of the alarms. Twenty-two minutes after five on April ninth.

"But what if it's not a puzzle at all?"

Not a future point. Not a ticking time bomb. Not a secret. But a secret code.

It was crystal clear. What if he turned the numbers into letters? Twenty was the letter 't'. Two was a 'b'. Five was 'd'. April was the fourth month so that was an 'e'. And the ninth was an 'I'. Altogether that spelled 'B-e-d-i-t'.

"Now that is really idiotic."

He was just about to give up the dumb idea of a secret code when he realized that the twenty-two could be a single number instead of two separate ones. So that made the letters spell 'v-e-d-i'. That still didn't mean anything. But if he rearranged the time and date? He had his answer, finally.

"Ugh. Why that?"

D-i-v-e.

It was the worst possible message of all.

The Black Ribbon

Toy couldn't dive. Skipped that lesson. All of them, really. When he watched the other kids plunge headfirst into the pool he was envious. From under the safety of his towel on the pool deck Toy watched them get their ribbons on the last day. Some of the kids celebrated by jumping off the high tower. Horrendously tall. He doubted that he could even climb the steel stairs let alone jump off.

He was afraid he'd get to the edge of the high platform and lose his balance, tumbling over the side and smacking the water. The coyote in the Roadrunner cartoons. Getting hurt never crossed his mind. Everyone laughing at him was the real problem. He pictured their twisted faces so vividly that for a minute it might have been an actual memory.

Fragments of the past were getting easily mistaken for others he was simply afraid might happen. He was pretty certain that he heard one of the kids that jumped off the tower say, "I touched the bottom. The bottom." The kid waved around the small rock that the lifeguard left in the deep end for someone to prove they made it. But his memory of the rock was that it was too large to hold in one hand.

The holes in his memory were like the ones in the carpet. It felt like his recall was baiting him. Unreliable. The only consistent thing in his days since the water came was the black ribbon. Looking down from his perch the ribbon was waving at him. Taunting.

"We'll see. I'm coming down there to get to the bottom of this."

The something under the water needed to be dealt with. Message delivered. The fear of diving underwater was rising in his stomach and he had to swallow it back down. It wasn't courage but there was no one else to do it. A first-timers problem. Momndad used to say there was a first time for everything. The person who did something for the first time, like ride the Ferris wheel for three weeks in a row was forced to figure things out on the fly.

He hoped that the constant haziness in his head was how the first astronaut felt sitting in the rocket before liftoff. Hyper-tuned to nothing but the water Toy was ready to act. All these days he had been taking things from the surface of the water without really thinking about what was going on below. He had seen the black ribbon and it was clearly growing. All of his adventures were nothing but a waste. And Cyril paid for it.

With the ribbon in full sight he could deny nothing. There were no more choices so everything else had to be put aside. Buried. His fear of putting his face in the water had to be submerged. He started to think about how he avoided blowing bubbles in the pool at swim lessons to keep his face dry.

"Stop thinking."

He recalled how the swim instructor was indifferent to Toy's worry about drowning.

"Stop it."

Toy pictured the time he almost drown in a pool.

"S.T.O.P."

That wasn't even a real memory. It wasn't in a pool. It was in the bathtub. Upstairs. He was trying out the new scuba mask Momndad brought him. He didn't want to chance it for the first time in the river or even a pool so he had tried the tub. He tried to push the plastic bathtub boats from his mind, the ones he wanted to see from underwater like sunken ships. It was the next best thing to scuba diving. He ran the bath to the very top then strapped the mask on tight. It covered his nose so he could only inhale through his mouth. His nose was totally blocked. It felt weird. Like suffocating. He concentrated hard on breathing only through his mouth, sitting in the full tub. Then with one huge gulp of air Toy thrust his face into the tub. His eyes were closed tight and it was an awkward feeling to have his head underwater. Everything sounded hollow. He was so nervous he forgot to open his eyes so he started the whole process over again.

He sat up in the tub, wiping water from his mouth and

flinging back his long black hair. Trying a second time he took in a gulp of air and held it but started to feel lightheaded so he sat up one more time. He wanted to get the most time underwater so he planned to take a huge gulp of air and then quickly submerge his face. Except he opened his mouth wide on the way down and swallowed a massive gulp of water. His lungs were immediately on fire as if he had drained the bath in one shot. He straightened up in a flash, coughing uncontrollably. Water was coming out of his nose and he jumped out of the bath with a single motion, slipping on the wet tiles. His feet flew up in the air and he hit his head. Somehow nobody heard the noise or they chose to ignore it. He toweled off and got into his pajamas, then put the scuba mask in the back of his bedroom closet. It was probably still there.

He wished he had that mask now. Even if he wanted to dive under the water he simply didn't know how. The high tower was real diving. He used to imagine climbing the pool's fence at night after closing time so he could jump off the high platform while no one was around. But he knew it was impossible. Doubly impossible because the fence was too tall to climb and there was no guarantee he wouldn't lose his nerve.

But everything was different at the Ferris wheel. There was no one around anymore and that was the one thing he had going for him. "No matter what happened at least I won't look like a fool."

There was something under the water. Whatever it was, he himself had figured it out while in one of his states and tried to communicate it to his waking self. He was going to have to face his fear. But it didn't make getting into the water any easier. Standing on the roof of the submerged gondola all of a sudden felt like the moment before swim lessons were about to start. The class gathered at the broad top stair in the corner of the outdoor pool. The beige tiled step was under a few inches of water, so Toy was already cold before he got all the way in. He took a few more steps down and right away the water was up to his chest. If he stepped any further into the shallow end he was sure the water would be over his head. What kind of shallow end was that? He thought that the mom*n*dads who dug the pool made a mistake about the depth because they hadn't counted on how short Toy was. He would drown in the shallow end before anybody realized. With plenty of prompting from the instructor, Toy stepped all the way into the shallow end. The other kids in the class stood with water up to their chests but for Toy it was touching his chin. This meant that at every moment he was a mouthful away from drowning.

Shaking his head to make the memories go away, he sat down on the edge of the gondola roof with his legs in the water. It was just as cold as the pool where he quit the lessons. Pushing away some of the plastic carpet to make himself a space, he wondered once again why he was going into the water so willingly. And then he just slipped in all at once, before his brain knew what he was doing. Still holding onto the gondola cage with one hand, his legs kicked instinctively. He really was sorry about putting the snorkel mask in the closet because he needed to see what was going on underneath. Sharply, he thrust his face into the water and opened his eyes. It burned. Salt water took some getting used to. He lifted his head out and thrust it in again, being sure to take a breath at the appropriate time. This time he was able to get down a little further and with his eyes open he could definitely see a problem.

Wisps of the black ribbon extended deep under the water. It was coming from very far below and so he was going to have to do much more than put his face in to solve the problem. He surfaced and took a huge breath. Letting go of the gondola to push himself under he found his thin body just floated on the surface. Getting up some courage, he willed himself beneath the surface waves only to float on his stomach like a beach ball.

"This is getting nowhere." Tiring, he climbed onto the watery gondola roof to figure things out.

Since he had never been below the surface of any water, it was all strange. He could hold his breath for ages above the water. In moments like these when he was angry around Mom*n*dad he could hold his breath for ages until he was blue in the face and gave up only when they shouted, "you'll pop a blood vessel in your head if you don't stop." Sadly, he'd never tried it below the water. In fact, it looked like holding air in his lungs was part of the problem. It was making him fill up like a balloon. The bodies that rose sputtering to the surface. So, Toy reasoned that he could finally sink if he dove in with a big breath and slowly let it out as he kicked towards the bottom of the new sea. But to make the plan work he guessed that he needed some real speed. He needed to jump into the water from high up like he saw the kids do at the pool tower. The high tower. There was no choice but to climb up to his gondola and jump.

The clamber to his perch felt strange for the very first time. Toy's pulse was racing despite the fact that he had become so accustomed to hanging out on the gondola roof for hours at a time. But now that he had to step off it into empty space, he was shaking. If he jumped far enough away from the Ferris wheel he would hit nothing on the way down except water, but if he slipped on takeoff there was a really good chance he'd hit one of the metal beams. The takeoff became his primary worry, not the landing. Just the fall. He had no solid plan for what was going to happen once he hit the liquid.

"Right about now would be time for some good old insurance." He didn't laugh. He only focused on what was going on at the bottom, under the Ferris wheel.

He closed his eyes and stopped thinking. In a single motion he opened his eyes and leaped into the air. There was a split second where his stomach darted up into his mouth, like it did on the Ferris wheel for his first time. Then, before he knew it he hit the water. It happened so fast that he didn't have time to take in a full breath. It would have to be enough, he thought, as he broke through the surface feet first, dropping like a stone.

The undersurface was terrifying but amazing. Barnacles covered the metal beams, hiding the coloured paint. Tiny fish swam in circles around the beams. The structure of the Ferris wheel beneath the surface had become a miniature ecosystem. The fish were happy and unaware. They swam in circles, fluidly

106

joining and splitting from groups with zero effort. Everyone belonged.

Then, Toy saw the black ribbon. It was coming from the very bottom of the Ferris wheel. Using the metal beam to pull himself deeper he saw that the black ribbon was coming from a large metal tank under the Ferris wheel. The tank was leaking from the seam of a round door the size of a watermelon. The tank was not cracked but it seemed as if the door wasn't fully closed. That was where the leak was coming from. Toy tried to push on the lever to fully close the door and stop the leak but it wouldn't budge. The lever was oily. He slipped off twice before heading back to the surface.

Suddenly things came into sharp focus. Oil coming from a very large tank under the Ferris wheel had been slowly leaking for days. If it kept leaking, it would ruin the habitat of fish and other sea animals that had grown up around the underwater base. Toy wasn't strong enough to push the level to its fully closed position to stop the leak. Then he stopped to think.

He asked himself if ignoring the ribbon would change his life. He was still eating from the bags and bottles of food that swirled around in the carpet. Was he immune to what was going on under the water? Sea water wasn't drinkable anyway so what difference did it make if it was polluted with oil? He didn't need to go swimming in it. Did he have a responsibility to fix something that wouldn't benefit him? There was no one around to look at him sideways. Nobody to tell him what to do.

Why was it so hard to think?

"Too bad those fish didn't have an insurance policy," he joked.

Insurance. He could be the insurance policy for the tiny fish. They'd never know he was the one that shut off the oil. "They don't even know it's there or they would have left long ago so somebody has to protect them."

One thing was for sure, if he did nothing then the oil would continue to leak in the water, exterminating all of the fish. But by protecting them he wondered who was really benefitting from the insurance. Insurance wouldn't prevent a bad thing from happening like your house burning down. It was supposed to build you a new house. So, if the insurance companies failed and were unable to put things back the way they were after a disaster then something was terribly wrong. For small things to work, like building a new house after a tornado, the big things had to stay the same. The big things were under massive strain. Runaway change. Toy had a chance to change all that.

"I can't imagine how one small change in this little part of the sea will matter. But it feels big to me."

The last thing to consider was how in the world was he going to manage to get to the bottom long enough to close the door, and with enough force. Jumping back into the water to try the same thing again was not going to work. He had to try something different. He wasn't strong enough to push the lever down by himself and he wasn't heavy enough in the water if he threw his whole weight on it either. What did he have that was heavy enough to move the lever? Nothing in the gondola would work. But under the water were some large rocks that he might use to knock the lever back into position. If he could lift one.

The first thing he needed was rope. And he had plenty of that. Even though his longest length of rope was lost with Cyril there was so much of it he had pulled from the carpet over the days. He tied a few of them together to make a single very long rope, and wrapped one end around his waist and fastened the other to metal beam x-33. The plan was to jump down to the ocean floor, unwrap the rope from his waist and tie it around one of the biggest rocks.

"The rock weighs less in the water just like I do."

The plan was to pull the rock up and then drop in onto the lever, closing it forever with a controlled smash. Simple.

"Not so easy," he said after returning to the surface. He had tied the rope to a large rock but couldn't lift it. Too heavy. In a panic, he couldn't believe he had come this far only to be stopped by a lack of muscle. "How can I lift something this heavy?"

"Pulling the rope straight up isn't going to work. But if I

loop it over the beam above my perch then I can tie something equally heavy to the free end of the rope. But I don't have anything equally as heavy as the rock. I know," Toy said cleverly "another rock". But then he realized that would never work. He had no possessions in the gondola except food.

"The food. Yes." Excitedly he gathered together all the heavy food and the water bottles into a heap and wrapped them in a large portion of tarp. Tying that massive bag to the rope's free end, Toy was proud of his engineering invention.

"All I have to do is pull down on the food side of the rope, and the rock will rise." It took a lot more effort than he expected but miraculously the food bag went down so that meant the rock was rising. He felt like a crane operator at a construction site, high up on his perch. He was just about to say that this was working remarkably well when the rope on the rock side of the pulley system got snagged on a little exposed bolt on the gondola's roof.

Toy was in an awkward position. Since both hands were holding the rope, he tried to kick at the snag to break it free. But all he got for the effort was a rope burn when the rock slipped a few inches as Toy lost his grip temporarily. He knew what he had to do.

"I can gather both sides of the rope together in one hand, prevent any more slipping and reach down with my free hand to untangle the rope." It was truly stuck. He seemed to have the rope secured and he needed both hands to untangle the snag. So he wrapped the rope around his leg to hold the rock in place.

Everything was balanced as he picked away at the snag when Toy heard a high pitched zinging sound. The rope suddenly came freed by itself and in one sweeping motion he was yanked into the air by his leg, thrown over the beam and pulled toward the water in pursuit of the rock. Entangled in the rope, he was dragged violently into the water and down to the bottom without time to take a deep breath.

He frantically tried to dislodge his leg from the rope. It wasn't working and he plummeted further under water. The rock hit the lever square on and jammed it squarely back into place.

But the rope wrapped itself around the lever and him. He was tied to the drum in some failed escape artist trick with his air almost run out.

Toy found himself in the awkward position of floating up-side down, tied to the lever by his leg. An absurdly thin helium balloon would not have looked more out of place. Instinctively he struggled harder but quickly figure out that it was useless. He would run out of air before he could untie the rope which was strangled around him like knotted string at the bottom of a drawer that, in defeat, a kitchen knife took care of.

The knife. Toy fumbled for the jackknife in his back pocket. Sawing at the rope while the air tried to explode from his lips he felt like a discarded birthday party balloon. He was looking at the uneaten cake while Momndad took a steak knife to the balloons once the last phone call cancelled the final invite. The depression in their rubbery skin giving away to the point of the knife. Everything cuts under the knife. Dozens of murdered birthday balloons scattered across the parquet floor. Toy cringed each time a balloon exploded as the knife pushed into the balloon's skin.

At the last minute the magician had to be called off with the excuse that Toy was sick. Each of the bright red balloons were stabbed and tossed into the trash while Toy wondered if he would still get a slice anyway.

At last the rope snapped with a muffled twang, sending Toy hurtling upward. He surfaced, coughing and gasping, eye to eye with the one impossible plastic bottle. Empty except for a single photo.

–

Toy threw himself onto the bench inside his perch, too tired to change out of his soaking wet clothes. The emergency hatch framed the sky. A new smell was in the air, something less grimy. He conceded it was possibly in his imagination. Wishful thinking. After a while he sat up with the bottle still in his hand, and looked out across the water. He thought of the genie being in this last bottle filled with a familiar trinity. He wondered if the three wishes still counted.

The carpet hadn't changed but there were little splashes from the fish jumping. He sat in silence a long time focused on the horizon and the splashes. For a time he thought be might be falling into another state, and suddenly worried he might never slip out again. But then it occurred to him that he swam, dived and even fell into the water without once entering one of his states. Something else had changed. More than the carpet. What was under the carpet didn't own him anymore.

Getting back to business as the sun burned and heated up the ocean, Toy set about reeling in the large tarp of food. It was empty. Bottles that spilled into the ocean needed to be re-caught all over again. Only this time he was prepared for a different un-bottling. Unbottling Cyril. Toy wished for his swan.

"You were a good listener and you stuck by me."

Then he unbottled the big rock. The little blonde boy was etched in Toy's memory, refusing to wear away with time but stubbornly surfacing when he was least combative. The water was a constant reminder of the lost beach. One forever over the other. It took all this water for Toy to own up to being afraid of the past while still hanging on.

The last thing he was afraid of was to think about Momndad. He closed his eyes and held the bottle in both hands. He held the third wish in his mouth, parting his dry lips as if to speak.

He could still see them standing there holding each other in their final embrace, waiting for Toy by the Ferris wheel. Waiting. They waited. He could feel it in his stomach. They never left but wanted only to see their boy until the very last moment. His tears were unbottled. A stream of more tears than could fill the bottle, mingling with the ocean. The tears Toy refused to shed for every other thing that was ever bottled up. He buried his head into his hands clutching the bottle. He was jolted by the alarm on his watch. It was a reminder he no longer needed. At last he wiped away the tears and thought about tomorrow. Tomorrow. Tomorrow he would get around to making that raft out of those bottles.

# ACKNOWLEDGEMENT

Writing this story meant that I was at times set adrift in an ocean of uncertainty and getting out of it was only possible because my family was my anchor. In particular I was guided by my daughter Haley who provided character insights and plot points. Early readers John Edmondson, Carolyn Nesbitt-Jerman and John Jerman gave support that would otherwise have caused me to pack it in. My own parents and sister were a constant source of inspiration that I turned to as I mined my past while looking to write into the very near future.

# ABOUT THE AUTHOR

## Barry Magrill

Barry Magrill is an artist, educator, and environmentally conscious citizen. He lives in Richmond, British Columbia with his family less than three blocks from the rising ocean.